WILD WIDOW OF WOLF CREEK

With two kids to raise, a ranch to run and no hired hands to help her, Kate Preston's troubles were increasing — but then Larry & Stretch came to Wolf Creek. The footloose drifters did not take kindly to hard cases preying on a defenceless widow. Within twenty-four hours of their arrival, they had notched up quite a score — seven men beaten up, three killed and one wounded in a violent shootout — and that was only the beginning!

MARSHALL GROVER

WILD WIDOW OF WOLF CREEK

A Larry & Stretch Western

Complete and Unabridged

LINFORD
Leicester

First published in Australia in 1981

First Linford Edition
published May 1995
by arrangement with
Horwitz Publications Pty Limited
Australia

Copyright © 1981 by Marshall Grover
All rights reserved

British Library CIP Data

Grover, Marshall
    Larry & Stretch: wild widow of Wolf Creek.
    —Large print ed.—
    Linford western library
    I. Title II. Series
    823 [F]

    ISBN 0–7089–7702–2

Published by
F. A. Thorpe (Publishing) Ltd.
Anstey, Leicestershire

Set by Words & Graphics Ltd.
Anstey, Leicestershire
Printed and bound in Great Britain by
T. J. Press (Padstow) Ltd., Padstow, Cornwall

This book is printed on acid-free paper

1

Rough Rescuers

WITH mixed feelings, four prominent identities of Detlow, Colorado, viewed the departure of two tall riders. Those riders, straddling a sorrel and a pinto, were slowly retreating to the northern outskirts of that progressive, well-settled town, packrolls secured, saddlebags well-filled. Messrs Lawrence Valentine and Woodville Emerson, better known as Larry and Stretch, were on their way out, never to return, and the four leading locals were relieved, intrigued, wistful, amused and profoundly impressed; mixed feelings was putting it mild.

"They were here a whole week," mused Coombes, the town marshal. "But they never saw the insides of my jail and there wasn't one brawl nor a shot fired in anger."

"I call that a miracle," declared Homer Vicks, editor of the Detlow 'Guardian'.

"Yeah, a miracle," nodded Coombes. "Almost every other town they've shown their faces, there's been strife, upheaval and mayhem."

"On the grand scale," frowned Elias Mohler, mayor of Detlow. "At least that's what Homer claims. Personally, I never heard of Valentine and Emerson till they rode into town seven days ago."

"You can believe everything I've ever published about the Texas Hell-Raisers," Vicks assured him. "No journalist needs to exaggerate their exploits. I've published nothing but the truth." He added, with a wry grin, "But the truth about those trouble-shooters always sounds like exaggeration."

"I liked them," muttered the fourth man. "I really mean that. They were friendly and co-operative — you couldn't meet two friendlier characters. Paid

2

all bills without protest, paid for all damages. Honestly, fellers, I have nothing but praise for them. But — oh, hell! Am I glad they've gone!"

He had good cause to feel this way. His name was Francis P. Harrigan and he was owner and manager of Detlow's best hotel, the Rialto in the heart of town. Upon their arrival, the notorious Lone Star Hellions had checked into his establishment, paying in advance for a week's rental of the most luxurious accommodation available, what he called the Senatorial Suite. His new guests had then proceeded to throw a party; that party hadn't broken up until around 3 o'clock this morning.

Detlow would never forget the seven-day bacchanale. When it came to hospitality, the drifters tended to be indiscriminate or, as Harrigan had put it, democratic to a fault. All stratas of Detlow society were more than welcome to stop by, drink and eat their fill — or more — and stay

3

as long as they wished. For the first time, Harrigan had seen the local lowlife disporting themselves in his handsomely-appointed lobby, dining room and the Senatorial Suite. Detlow's doctor, two lawyers and resident judge found themselves rubbing shoulders with stablehands, saloon swampers, tinhorns, deadbeats and ladies of easy virtue. Laid on lavishly were all varieties of booze, including champagne, also the best food Detlow had to offer, not only roast beef, venison and chicken prepared by the Rialto's chef, but chop suey brought in from a Chinese restaurant. All this and music too. Any local capable of producing a lively tune, any guitar-strumming layabout from the Mexican quarter, any or all members of Detlows' brass band, had an open invitation to stop by, fetch their instruments, their appetites and, of course, their thirsts. Seven days of noisy revelry were at last ended. And now, at the Rialto, the cleaning up process was under way.

"A good time was had by all," grinned Vicks.

"Well, sure," nodded the mayor. "And I'm thankful nobody suffered any serious injury."

"And I appreciate the extra business," said Harrigan.

"All Detlow appreciates the extra business," drawled Vicks. "I checked with the local storekeepers and I can tell you how much the big spree cost Valentine and his buddy. Well, a rough estimate anyway."

"Couple thousand bucks," guessed the marshal.

"Closer to three thousand," said Vicks.

"Well, let's not forget they financed roof repairs and a new harmonium for the Baptist chapel," said Mayor Mahler, "as well as making a heavy donation to our new orphanage."

"Damn generous of 'em," Harrigan conceded. "Taking that into consideration, I guess we should overlook the — uh — more unfortunate incidents."

5

"Such as some deadbeat picking my pocket," frowned Mohler.

"And Lulu Seigel — that fat old whore — getting a skinful of gin and passing out on the Methodist minister's front porch," grouched Coombes." And some joker stealing a wheel. Damn it, that was the rear wheel of the finest surrey in these parts."

"Owned by the manager of the First National Bank," nodded Harrigan. "Mighty unfortunate."

"Was that wheel ever recovered?" Vicks thought to enquire.

"Somebody found it on the roof of the Western Union office," Coombes reported. "How it ever got there is anybody's guess. Some men don't know their own strength when they're fired up on high-class booze. We've had one helluva hectic week, gents, but . . . " He shrugged and chuckled softly, "I guess we're agreed it might've been worse."

"Could've been far worse," the Guardian editor assured him, "and far more destructive."

6

"From the minute they rode into town, I guessed who they were," sighed Coombes. "I've been expecting trouble ever since. To me, they never looked better than when they saddled up and quit town. I'll sleep easy tonight — for the first time since they arrived."

"Surely Nate's an alarmist," Mohler suggested to Vicks.

"No." The newspaper man shook his head. "Every lawman fears the worst when Valentine and Emerson enter his bailiwick."

"How could they be as violent as Nate says?" wondered Mohler. "Two fiddlefoots so friendly, so generous?"

"Well, I'm not saying they're friendly and generous and violent at the same time," shrugged Vicks. "You want to know the truth about them? I can tell you. Any frontier newspaperman can tell you. After a few years of reporting their deeds of daring, we're well-qualified, believe me."

"Deeds of daring sounds like story-book stuff," protested Harrigan.

"Listen to Homer," advised the marshal. "He's not fooling."

"They've been wandering all over the frontier since the war ended," Vicks told them. "They were raised in the Texas Panhandle and their ancestry was predominantly Irish, but they're so damn nomadic they might as well be full-blood Navajos. Never could settle anywhere. Ask them what they want of life and they'll tell you they crave to drift along quietly, stay lazy and steer clear of danger and strife and just mind their own business. They could be absolutely sincere about that, for all I know. Personally, I don't care either way. All I know is they're a journalist's dream come true. I'm ready to believe they aren't trouble-makers, of course . . ."

"I'm near ready to believe that," frowned the marshal, "now that I've met 'em."

"And partaken of their hospitality," grinned Harrigan.

"But they're trouble just the same,"

declared Vicks. "They attract violence and conflict wherever they go. Maybe they're directly responsible or maybe it just happens. One thing to their credit — they're no threat to law-abiding folk. But outlaws, hard cases, thieves, killers? Their natural enemies. They seem to have this deep-rooted, instinctive hostility toward the lawless. And believe me, the feeling is mutual."

"Outlaw-fighters," mused the mayor.

"That's what they do best," Vicks assured him. "I wouldn't attempt to estimate the number of desperadoes they've fought and defeated. I doubt if anybody else could offer an accurate figure. It would require a lengthy research of the files of the army, the U.S. marshal's office, the Pinkertons and a great many county sheriffs."

"Here in Detlow, I thought sure you'd have a budget for a dozen special deputies," the marshal told the mayor. "When the local cattlemen started drifting in — and those roughneck minehands from the Yampa Ridge diggings — there'd just have to be a riot, I told myself. In every other town, that's what usually happens. Some proddy ranch-hand or a lickered-up miner hankers to build himself a reputation by tangling with a couple famous scrappers and all hell breaks loose." He sighed heavily, and grateful. "But it didn't happen here."

"How could it?" shrugged Harrigan. "What cowpoke or minehand would pick a fight with a stranger who invites him to eat and drink all he can hold?"

"The moment our local bully-boys arrived, Valentine and Emerson were inviting them to join the party," grinned Vicks. "Every roughneck accepted the invitation, and that, my friends, was the miracle. A wild party it was . . . "

"The wildest," said Mohler, wincing.

"Rowdy and prolonged, but unmarred by bloodshed," said Vicks.

"Yes, I'm sure we're all agreed it could've been far worse," said Harrigan. "Anyway you look at it, Detlow suffered no serious damage and quite a few of us showed a handsome profit."

"How could a couple of drifters be so well-heeled?" wondered Mohler.

"I asked them about that," said Vicks. "They didn't realize I'm a newspaperman because I deemed it discreet to keep my profession a secret. So, with me, they were quite frank. Seems they're gambling luck has been running high in recent times. And wait till you hear this . . . " He chuckled softly. "A thick bankroll is their idea of bad trouble. Their needs are simple, so they're leery of affluence. A few hundred is ample for the likes of them, Valentine told me. By the time they reached this town, they had the spending itch."

"Hankered to get rid of their excess wealth, you mean?" grinned Harrigan.

"That's why they threw a party — for the whole town?" Mohler asked incredulously.

"Sounds far-fetched, I agree," said Vicks. "But you have to admit they achieved their purpose."

Still solvent to the tune of some $900, the compulsive drifters crossed the border and entered the territory of Wyoming five days later. They were idling their mounts through brushy and rock-strewn terrain some distance from any marked trail and, within the next few minutes, would behold a scene that would start their scalps crawling and chill their blood. Until then, their mellow mood would prevail. They were content, now that their bankroll was reduced to a less spectacular figure, at least on their standards.

Larry Valentine, the thinking half of this much-traveled partnership, puffed on a thinly-rolled cigarette and let his clean-limbed sorrel amble easy. Dark-haired and alert-eyed, handsome in a battered, heavy-jawed way, he was a brawny Texan whose muscle-power was still formidable; it would take more than 20 years of knight-errantry and twice as many battle wounds to slow him down.

Rigged like his sidekick in travel-stained range clothes, Woodville Emerson, nicknamed Stretch for his uncommon height, was always the guileless one, an easy-going tagalong content to leave the brain-work to the more mentally agile Larry, but a sturdy ally even so. Though his frame was spare and gangling, he could match Larry for brute strength. He packed twice as much Colt as Larry, being ambidextrous with handguns; the second .45 was holstered at his left hip. Homely as they come was the Emerson, with his tousled blond thatch, too-wide mouth, too-long chin and ears that stuck out like jug-handles, but he had his own peculiar kind of appeal. And he was a man just bound to win attention. In an era when six-footers weren't all that plentiful, he stood six and a half feet tall, which made him three inches taller than burly Larry.

"What'd we need with all that dinero anyway?" he drawled, and not for the first time since their quitting Detlow, Colorado. "Better'n thirty-eight hundred bucks we had — and what could we do with so much?"

"If we'd hung onto it any longer, we'd likely have lost every last dime of it," opined Larry. "We'd have gotten robbed. Or maybe I'd have lost it all in an all-night poker party."

"Had us a time in Detlow, didn't we?" grinned Stretch. "Plenty booze, plenty socializin' and celebratin' — and never no trouble."

"Beats fightin' every time," Larry said wistfully.

To which the taller Texan warmly agreed,

"Ain't that the truth."

As on so many occasions in their hectic career, the carefree mood gave way to nerve-wracking tension with startling suddenness. They guided their mounts around a brush-clump and there it was directly ahead, a sight that caused them to jerk back on their reins and gape in shock.

The barefoot boy, in patched overalls

and homemade shirt was tiny, a freckled redhead chuckling gleefully and clinging to one end of a five-feet long sapling rod. He was withdrawing his pole from a cluster of boulders, having disturbed the reptile lurking there. Now, the rattlesnake was half-wound around the end of the rod. The boy was waggling the rod and the rattler raising its head to strike at him when Stretch regained the power of speech and yelled a warning.

"Drop it and jump clear, kid!"

Instead of dropping his find, the boy flashed the horsemen a cheery grin. Larry loosed an oath, emptied his holster and cocked, aimed and triggered all in one swift blur of movement. The .45 slug rendered the rattler headless. Only then did the boy let go of his pole. Only then did Larry's scalp stop crawling.

Stretch, a sentimentalist who had rarely met a child he didn't like, now suffered a delayed reaction. Sweating profusely, trembling, he slid from his pinto, tottered to a patch of grass and squatted crosslegged.

Larry mumbled another oath. Emotionally, he was tougher than his sidekick. He had become somewhat of a hard-boiled cynic in recent years, but was only human after all. He was panting heavily when he dismounted, delved into his saddlebag for a bottle and trudged across to flop beside Stretch. Since Appomattox, these veterans had survived more hair's breadth crises than they cared to recall, more fights to the death, more assaults to their nerves than Mr Average Man could experience in an entire lifetime. They had fought homicidal bandidos and scalp-hunting Indians and escaped fire, flood and even an avalanche or two. Frontier journalists claimed they had nerves of steel.

So much for the extravagant writings of newspapermen. The survivors of a hundred and one violent affrays could still be shaken, and badly. And this was one of those times. The bottle was uncorked. Stretch grabbed for it desperately and fed himself a badly needed shot, a long one. Larry, whose need was as great, did likewise.

They were still trembling as they fished out Durham-sacks. They made a hash of the simple, familiar chore of rolling and lighting cigarettes, spilling tobacco. Larry then focussed on the grinning little boy, tried to assume a stern expression, but failed. He could have bellowed a furious reprimand at an older child maybe. But this ginger-thatched sprig was so tiny, so pitifully young and vulnerable, standing there grinning his gap-toothed grin. He corked the bottle and crooked a finger. The boy advanced eagerly and hunkered between the unnerved giants.

"What . . . " Larry coughed smoke, winced and tried again. "What's your name, boy?"

It took the tall men several minutes to make sense of Jarvis Preston's childish, rambling prattle. He was

four, going on five, so too young
for school. Sure, he lived hereabouts.
With Mama and Sister Irma. Where
was his pa? In heaven, Mama says.
Wouldn't his ma be mad at him for
straying away like this?

"Guess so," shrugged Jarvis.

"You could've got yourself killed
— pokin' a stick at a snake," Larry
pointed out.

"He was a big'un," enthused Jarvis.

"Aw, hell," sighed Stretch. "Poor
little sprig — too young to savvy
the danger." He eyed Larry warily.
"You ain't gonna paddle his ass, are
you?"

"If I thought it'd do any good,"
muttered Larry. "But it wouldn't. He's
just too *young*."

He tried a few more questions. Was
Jarvis lost, or could he find his way
home? And how much time had passed
since he began this snake-hunt? Only
the last question was confusing to the
boy. He sure wasn't lost, could find his
way home easily. But, at his tender age,

time had little meaning. Then Stretch thought to ask.

"Did you sneak away before you ate or after?"

"After," grinned Jarvis.

"After what?" prodded Larry. "Breakfast — lunch . . . ?"

"Lunch." Jarvis was sure of the meal. "We had beans and tomato."

Larry dug out his watch, checked the time and grimaced.

"Three o'clock. His mother'll be frettin' up a storm."

"Best take him home," decided Stretch. "Jarvis boy, you sure you know the way?" The boy nodded eagerly. "Well, all right then. You want to ride double with me?"

Their nerves fortified with whiskey, the tall men felt equal to the chore of restoring the tiny runaway to the bosom of his family. In childish delight, the boy perched behind the taller Texan on the smart-stepping pinto. No danger of his falling; both small hands were hooked to the back of Stretch's shellbelt.

"Straight ahead?" asked Larry. Another eager nod from Jarvis. "Bueno. Let's get goin'."

The boy had strayed quite a distance. At intervals, while pushing northward, they sighted the small footprints on sandy patches. Through tall timber, around rockmounds and in and out of flowering brush they moved, traveling better than two miles and marveling at the stamina and adventurous spirit of the very young. Asked if the family home were in a town, the boy shook his head.

"Homestead?" prodded Stretch.

"We got cattle," offered Jarvis.

"Big herd, huh?" frowned Larry.

"Ma says more'n a hundred head," said Jarvis. "She can count and so can Irma. Me, I don't count so good."

"You'll learn how when you start goin' to school — if you live that long," muttered Larry. "You gonna mind what I told you? No more huntin' rattlers?"

"I never caught one before," grouched

Jarvis. "And now I got to quit."

"Smart hombre quits while he's ahead," Stretch assured him. To his partner, he remarked, "Sounds like a small spread. Just a hundred head."

"How many hired hands, Jarvis?" asked Larry.

"All gone now," shrugged Jarvis. He squinted with the effort of working his memory. "Used to be four. All gone now."

"So who runs the spread?" demanded Stretch.

"How many people at your place, boy?" prodded Larry.

"Just Ma and me and Irma," said Jarvis.

The Texans traded frowns when, some time later, they reached the bank of a slow-flowing creek. Jarvis casually identified it as Wolf Creek. He had forded it, but how? Though nowhere near flood level, the creek looked to be deep enough to be dangerous to a child so small. Home range was beyond the north bank; they could see grazing

21

cattle some 150 yards further on.

"You couldn't have crossed here, young feller," opined Larry, as they nudged the horses into the shallows.

The boy chattered on in his rambling, disjointed way, but now they were becoming used to the conversation of this tiny fellow-male a fraction their age. Apparently, some short distance downstream, the creek narrowed. There were, in Jarvis' words, 'plenty rocks for hopin' over'. This conjured up a mind-picture of the half-pint-sized runaway making the crossing by way of half-submerged rocks. And in his bare feet yet. One slip could have meant another reduction of the Preston family.

After fording Wolf Creek, they rode the south sector of Preston range and appraised the grazing herd. 100 head? Maybe. But a tally would take time. These were untended steers straying at will. Their brief glimpse of white horns and brown hides in the timber to the east and the brushy slopes to the west were more than enough proof the Preston bunkhouse was empty.

Dead ahead was the ranch-house, a single-storied structure. At this distance it seemed secure enough with its shingled roof and its shaded porch, smoke rising from a rock chimney. The other buildings, outhouses, the barn and bunkhouse, were situated east of the corrals. Yes, at this distance the Preston home did seem secure, the lazily spiraling smoke adding a tranquil effect. But, as they drew closer, they noted the four saddled horses tied to the hitchrail in front of the porch. This didn't seem to alarm young Jarvis, but it certainly surprised him.

"We don't get company, Ma says."

The ugly sounds reached them, when they had advanced another twenty yards. They reined up, traded quick glances and began dismounting. Added to the noise of a plate shattering were the harsh male voices, one raised in raucous laughter, another yelling obscene curses. And, rising higher, the sound most like to arouse their ire — a woman's strident scream.

Larry was out of his saddle already and running. Stretch swung down, deposited Jarvis on his feet and pushed a stern finger into his startled face.

"You stay *right here* and you don't budge *an inch* — savvy?"

"Why's Ma hollerin?" fretted the boy.

"That's what we're gonna find out," growled Stretch, as he took off at a loping run.

He was close behind his partner when they crossed the front yard. Scorning the steps, they vaulted up to the porch and charged through an open doorway to find themselves in the ranch kitchen and confronting a scrawny, unkempt man taken aback by their sudden arrival. Behind him, sounds of a scuffle issued from another open doorway; the woman was screaming again.

Rallying from his surprise, the scrawny man transferred a half-empty bottle from his right hand to his left, the better to grope for his holstered pistol. The Texans charged and the pistol stayed holstered. Larry, first to reach the man, seized him by his right arm and swung him off his feet. Yelling, the hard case hurtled across the kitchen and through the outer doorway. A porch-post checked his rush; he struck it face-first and collapsed, while the Texans barged into the parlor.

This room was in worse shape than the kitchen. The sofa, a table and two chairs were overturned. Through a red haze of fury, Larry caught a blurred impression of the woman, her auburn hair streaming about her bare shoulders. The intruders had stripped her of her gown and now, in nought but threadbare underwear, she defended herself gamely against three cursing assailants. The bulkiest of the three, his face scored by her fingernails, was raising a hand to strike at her, his cohorts gripping the woman's arms, when the Texans charged again.

Stretch swung a boot and the would-be woman-beater went down, his legs kicking from under him. One of the other men let go of the woman and swung a blow that caught Stretch full in the face. Stretch made a growling sound and retaliated with a slamming, ferocious belly-blow and a swinging uppercut, while Larry rained blows on the fourth man, hard, fast, punishing blows to face and body, not letting up until his victim sagged whimpering and the man with the scratched face lurched upright and tried grabbing at his throat. Her back to the wall, the woman stared aghast at an exhibition of brute strength she would long remember. Not only did Larry seize his attacker; he lifted him easily as if he weighed mere ounces and carried him struggling from the room. Stretch, after politely touching his hat brim to her, grasped the other two by an arm and a leg and followed. She stumbled to the connecting doorway and, incredulously, watched the tall men hurl the intruders from the kitchen entrance one by one, sending them flying over the porch-rail to crash into the yard.

She retreated to her bedroom, donned a robe and, moments later, appeared on the porch. By then, the four were dazedly picking themselves up and the tall men watching them from atop the porch steps. Still with his eyes on them, Larry questioned her.

"You know these polecats? They from some other ranch hereabouts?"

"Never saw them before!" she panted. "They're strangers. They just rode in and — and saw I was alone here — and tried to . . . "

"All right," scowled Larry. "You don't have to say it. Plain enough what they'd have done to you."

"If you're ever in doubt . . . " She sighed heavily and slumped against the front wall, "just ask *me*."

"Climb on them horses and ride — and I mean right out of this territory," ordered Larry.

"Just vamoose," urged Stretch. "Don't

27

back-talk us and don't make no rash moves. First skunk tries pullin' a gun — we'll blow hell through all four of you."

"I hope they do that," declared Larry, and there was death in his eyes.

The battered and bloody womanizers studied the tall men a long moment before slipping their reins and struggling astride their horses. They turned the animals and began moving south towards the creek, past the gaping boy who, at a nod from Larry, scampered for the yard. The woman at once chided him.

"Where've you *been*, Jarvis? You ran away again — after I've told you . . . !"

"I don't hold with young'uns runnin' away from home," frowned Larry.

"Specially a peewee like Jarvis," muttered Stretch.

"But this time was lucky for you," Larry told the woman. "We found the little feller and brought him home. If we hadn't . . . " He grimaced and shrugged apologetically. "All right, forget I said that."

"I'm not about to forget anything," she murmured. "Jarvis, you wash your face at the well. Pail's full. Then you go play in the bunkhouse while I talk to these gentlemen." As the boy ambled to the well, she identified herself. "Name's Kate Preston."

"Our pleasure, ma'am," nodded Stretch, doffing his Stetson. "My partner is Valentine and I'm Emerson."

"If you'll wait a moment while I — put on another gown — we could talk here on the porch," she offered.

"We'll wait," said Larry.

But they followed her into the house and, after she disappeared through the connecting doorway, began doing their best to set the kitchen to rights. Obviously the struggle had begun here. The floor was littered with potatoes and carrots, the potatoes half-peeled, the carrots half-scraped. Spilled water and the broken pieces of a basin indicated the widow had been preparing supper when intruded upon. There was little they could do but pick up the mess and right overturned chairs. Stretch found a broom and was sweeping broken glass and crockery out the doorway when Kate Preston appeared, her well-knit figure garbed in checked gingham, her hair drawn to a knot behind her neck.

"You didn't have to do that," she protested.

"Beats hangin' around doin' nothin'," retorted Larry.

And now he sized her up and pegged her for what she was, a woman in her late 20's and forced to go it alone, still passably attractive, especially with that mane of auburn hair and the wide-set hazel eyes, the straight nose, generous mouth and firm chin, but toilworn and, right now, still shaky.

At her insistence they moved out to the porch. She seated herself. Larry took the other chair while his partner perched on the porch-rail. Studying her more closely, Larry cursed under his breath; there was a bruise at her jawline.

"Jarvis up to any mischief when you came on him?" she demanded. "Go ahead, tell me."

"Heck, no . . . " began Stretch.

"I can take it — believe me I can take it," she assured them. "If I don't hear it from you, Jarvis'll tell me. He's a half-pint of trouble, that child, getting into mischief all the time. But he never lies to me."

"No way you can corral him?" challenged Larry.

"That question proves you're a bachelor," she sighed. "A family man wouldn't ask. How do you keep a little boy cooped up after he's learned how to walk and run? There's no way."

"We found him the other side of the creek," said Larry.

"Oh, Lord." She raised a hand to her brow. "He crossed the creek again."

Gently, but firmly, and with his wary eyes on her troubled face, Larry reported the circumstances of their

31

finding the tiny runaway. Her face lost some of its color.

"I'm sorry," he shrugged. "But that's how it was."

"You'd think two kids wouldn't be too much for a widow to handle, wouldn't you?" she asked.

"Well . . . " he began.

"The kids I could handle," she declared. "But how can I run a ranch without help? Since Joe died and the hired hands ran out on us, there's only been Irma and Jarvis and me." She gestured wearily. "Better than a hundred and fifty good steers out there. Unless I can hire help, how am I going to keep them on home range and out of the timber? Cattle are as much trouble as Jarvis with his wander-itch. Only one thing for it, I've just got to find another husband, get myself married again — and soon — before it's too late." She eyed them hopefully and made her offer and they doubted the evidence of their ears. "Listen, how'd you like to stay on and help run the

Wolf Creek Ranch? And, if one of you wants to marry me and settle down, that's all right. I'm good and ready."

Stretch's reaction was eloquent and ungraceful. He started convulsively, overbalanced and toppled from the rail.

2

Set-up

IN recent times, Larry Valentine had often remarked,

'If a man keeps driftin', he'll meet all kinds.'

The remark did seem to fit this situation. For the second time that afternoon he was spilling tobacco in the act of rolling a cigarette, a reaction not as spectacular as his partner's, but just as irritating. While he resumed his struggle with Bull Durham and cigarette paper, Stretch rose from the flower-bed in front of the porch, shook his head dazedly and trudged to the steps. In his present reduced condition, the top step seemed a safer perch than the porch-rail. He squatted there, frowning over his shoulder at Kate Preston, who grimaced indignantly and chided herself.

"I have to stop doing that. Doc Edwards warned me I'm trying too hard and no man wants to be rushed."

"Did you do it to Doc Edwards too?" Larry coldly enquired. "Propose at him — just like that?"

"Of course not," she frowned. "He's near fifty and been married for twenty-five years."

"Kate Preston, four men attacked you just a little while ago," he said grimly. "I don't believe you're lame-brained. You know what they'd have done . . ."

"They made it clear enough," she nodded.

"You saw my partner and me hurt 'em bad, and that was no purty sight for a woman," he declared. "By now, any other woman'd be tryin' to rest, tryin' to settle her nerves and still feelin' the shock of it all — and the hurt. But you? You wash your face, fix your hair, put on another gown and offer yourself to a couple hombres you never saw before. So what in tarnation kind of woman *are* you?"

She was ready with an answer, a long one, quite a speech in fact, and so vehement that he froze in the act of lighting his smoke.

"A *desperate* woman, Mister Valentine! Desperate because this ranch is all I have — plus two kids who have to be raised and some cattle, not a big herd, but prime, cattle that could bring top dollar if I could get them to the railhead. Desperate because we're so *defenceless* here! What kind of cowhands ride for the big spreads of Council Valley?" She gestured eastward. "You suppose they're all fine gentlemen, the kind who'd never think of taking advantage of a lone widow? Diamond Seven hands, Bible hands, Rocking B hands, they come by on their way to the county seat — all of 'em with the same itch!"

"You sayin' this wasn't the first time . . . ?" began Larry.

"This was my closest call," she said

36

bitterly. "No buck ever got to tear my gown off before. I still have Joe's rifle and six-gun and plenty of ammunition. And I have to use it! That's how I protect myself when needs be!"

"Holy Hannah!" breathed Stretch.

"I can't hire help," she went on. "No way I can compete with those big outfits up in the valley. Mat McCord and the other ranchers are grazing thousands of beeves on their range and need all the help they can hire, bribe or bully. Every time a stranger, an out-of-work cowhand shows up in the county seat, he scarce gets time to cool his saddle before somebody's offering him a riding job. Mister McCord and his neighbors have friends in town keeping an eye out for new hands. You want to know how I lost the four good men used to work for us here? Two months after my husband died of pneumonia, there was a new gold strike across the border in Colorado . . . ."

"Your men got gold-fever and just quit on you?" frowned Larry.

"That was a rough time for me," she assured him. "You want to know *how* rough? Joe died three months before I bore Jarvis. Well . . . " She shrugged and grimaced, "That was quite a time back. I respect Joe's memory, but I can't mourn him for the rest of my life, can I? Only one way I can keep this spread working and raise my son and daughter. I have to marry again. I need a husband around the place, a man strong enough to protect me. And Irma. She's only seven, but growing fast. By the time she's fifteen or so, *she'll* need protection."

"What's it called, the county seat?" demanded Larry.

"Cormack," said Kate. "Seat of Bridger County."

"So there has to be a county sheriff," said Larry.

"Sure," she nodded. "An old deputy name of Dubb."

"The law's supposed to look out for decent folks," Stretch pointed out.

"What can one lawman do?" she

shrugged despondently. "Must be better than a hundred hot-blooded cowpokes ride for the Council Valley outfits — and I'm on their route to Cormack. If Sheriff Holbrook tried tangling with them . . . "

"That's what he's paid for," growled Larry. He finally got around to lighting his cigarette. Then, surveying her grimly, he began his warning. "Maybe marryin' again will make things easier for you, but this ain't the way. You can't just up and offer yourself to a doggone stranger. You don't have to be *that* desperate."

"How would you know?" she countered. "You never had such a problem."

"It's — uh — well — it's risky," Stretch said uneasily.

"You never saw us before," said Larry. "We could be bad medicine — on the run from the law."

"Or rustlers lookin' to steal your cattle," nodded Stretch.

"You could end up wed to some

jasper with a price on his head," warned Larry. "No matter how desperate you feel, you ought to be careful."

"And mighty particular," asserted Stretch. "On account of marriage is plumb permanent."

"You two I can trust," shrugged Kate.

"How d'you know?" challenged Larry.

"The way you roughed up those trail-tramps." She smiled wistfully and caressed her bruised jaw. "You'd have to be gentlemen — deep down — else you wouldn't have gotten so mad. I'm guessing you always get mad when you see a woman man-handled."

"It kind of irks us," Stretch admitted.

"So you aren't looking for a wife, Mister Valentine," she said. "But you're looking for work, right? And I can tell you and your friend are cattlemen. So what do you say? I need help and I can pay regular cowhands' wages."

"We'll think it over," said Larry, rising. "We're headed for Cormack now. I need to talk to the sheriff."

"It's west from here," she offered. "You travel my west quarter, stay right of the woody ridge and you'll come to the town-trail." As he quit the porch with his partner, she called after him. "Keep my offer in mind — please? I can afford to hire you. Joe had life insurance, so I'm not broke. Nor rich. But not broke."

The tall men were crossing the yard, headed back to where they had left their horses, when the three children, a boy and two girls, rode in from the west. The big mare, a docile animal, carried no saddle, just a bridle and her young lightweight customers. One of the girls, a pretty, dark-haired 7-year-old, dropped from the animal, and waved so-long.

"See you tomorrow, Irma," grinned the boy. "C'mon, ol' Ellie."

"Mama, we having company?" asked Irma Preston. She had lost interest in her friends and was appraising the rough-hewn strangers. "My! They're so *tall*!"

"The gentlemen are just leaving, honey," said Kate. "Mister Valentine, Mister Emerson, my daughter Irma."

"Our pleasure, little lady," acknowledged Larry and, despite his grim mood, he touched his hat-brim and showed the child an amiable grin.

"Well, howdy do, Miss Irma," beamed Stretch.

He won a giggle from Irma and a smile from her mother by doffing his Stetson and according her a bow. The child responded by curtseying and, as the Texans moved on, anger and sadness assailed them.

They were feeling it now, a natural resentment, a sense of outrage, that chivalry seemed to have died in this corner of Wyoming, that a woman could be rendered so vulnerable by widowhood, forced to defend herself with the weapons of her late husband.

While they were remounting, the taller Texan read his partner's mind.

"We'll be comin' back, huh? Hang around long enough to rally the strays and get 'em to feed-grass, do a little fixin' round the place?"

"We got nothin' better to do," muttered Larry. "Except brace that sheriff."

"You sound mean enough to spit in his eye," remarked Stretch, as they wheeled their horses and started westward.

"Lawman ought to earn his pay," growled Larry. "Least he could do was warn them Council Valley hands or maybe talk to their bosses." His jaw tightened. "If this badge-toter is squeamish, it might be me and you has to teach them skirt-chasers a lesson."

Around sundown, when they idled their mounts into that fast-growing Wyoming cowtown, they were thinking only of Sheriff Holbrook. The four rogues encountered so violently at the Wolf Creek spread were forgotten.

Cormack, in their eyes, was no better, no worse than a hundred and one cattle towns they had seen in their years of wandering. Passers-by showed little interest in them and the feeling was mutual until they paused to ask directions to the sheriff's office. The townman who directed them also relayed a job offer. Rocking B was hiring and they couldn't hope to ride for a better outfit. A half-block from their destination they were accosted by another local as intent on earning a commission; he tried to persuade them to sign on with Diamond 7.

"Like the widow-lady said," drawled Stretch, when they dismounted in front of the county jail. "Stranger don't get time to cool his saddle."

"She wasn't foolin'," nodded Larry.

The lawman on duty was no youngster, and that was an understatement. Straggly iron-grey hair hung to his shoulders, matching his full mustache and short beard. Bright blue eyes surveyed the strangers from a deeply-lined countenance while the gnarled paws worked on with practiced efficiency. He identified himself and they didn't need to over-exert their powers of observation to deduce that Deputy Sheriff Aaron Dubb had not always worn a badge. His jacket was of fringed buckskin. The battered hat hung near the gunrack sported a turkey-feather. And those gnarled paws worked lovingly on the chore of honing the points of arrows spilled from a quiver on the desk. Above the gunrack, a warbow of Sioux origin had pride of place.

"If you didn't used to be an Injun scout, old timer, I wasn't born in Texas," Stretch opined.

"You got smart eyes — considerin' you're some younger'n me," old Aaron said cheerfully. "Sure enough, boys, I've scouted for Crooks and Custer and even General Grant hisself. Couple hours 'fore Custer started for the Little Big Horn with the Seventh, durned if I didn't come down with a misery. Ended up in the fort infirmary. Ptomaine, the doc said.

"Better a bellyache than losin' your scalp," suggested Larry.

"Goes to prove a man never knows when his time'll come," drawled Aaron. "Somethin' I can do for you?"

"Lookin' for the sheriff," said Larry.

"He'll be with Mayor Archand," offered Aaron. "Less'n a quarter-hour ago, Cleave Archand come by and collected him, said as how he'd buy him a drink."

"Which saloon?" asked Larry.

"Didn't say." Aaron chuckled raspily. "And, in this here town, saloons is plumb plentiful. But you should complain? Worse places you could seek him. 'Least you get to keep your whistle wet."

"Might take us quite a time to find him, runt," frowned Stretch.

"Lookin' at you bucks, I just can't believe you're temperance," grinned Aaron.

"Ain't temperance, never have been, never will be," shrugged Stretch.

As they retreated to the law office doorway, Larry could not resist offering a suggestion.

"Fine-lookin' warbow you own. Purty arrows too. But, for keepin' the peace in a paleface town, a handgun's easier to tote."

The old man chuckled again, and abandoned his arrows and sharpening block long enough to cross-draw a pistol and exhibit it for their appraisal.

"Never was a trouble-maker back-talked me, not if he found his ornery self lookin' in the muzzle of this ol' shooter. Way back in 'forty-eight they pree-sented me with this fine Colt Dragon, the troops at Camp Scranton. Purty, huh?"

"Just beautiful," Stretch said admiringly.

"Some say I'm slowin' down," confided Aaron. "Well now, I'll allow the bones're creakin' and there's snow on the roof, but the shooting' eye's still good. I'm the only deputy Breck Holbrook got and I can tell you he ain't complainin' none."

"We believe you, Aaron," nodded Larry, as they moved out.

Leaving their horses tied to the

law office hitchrail, the newcomers began checking the many saloons along Cormack's main stem. After drawing a blank at the first three, they resigned themselves to a lengthy search and pressed on, unaware they had been sighted, recognized and marked for death by recent adversaries. The area they walked en route to the next saloon on Main Street's east side, Sharney's Bar, was well-lit. They were coming on slowly, unwittingly giving their would-be assassins ample time to prepare.

But twenty years of knight errantry had honed their reflexes and boosted their sixth sense. Almost in the act of nudging the batwings open and entering the barroom, they were on the alert, their instant wariness belied by their casual demeanor. The only visible customers were two aged locals sharing a table by the northside wall and the man slumped in the corner right of the entrance; his head was on the table and cradled in his arms and he looked to be sleeping.

While sauntering toward the bar, Larry noted the two old timers were gripping their booze, keeping their eyes averted and not budging an inch; he could have believed they weren't even breathing. The barkeep was wiping glasses, presenting an impassive exterior, but sweating. And the evening was cool. The proprietor, seated alone at a table near the bottom of the stairs, was spare of physique, elderly and garbed in sober black; he was dealing solitaire as though his life depended on it. Tension? Expectation? Danger? The Texans sensed it, smelt it, could almost taste it.

"'Evenin'," grunted the barkeep.

"'Evenin'," nodded Larry.

"What'll it be?" asked the barkeep.

"Couple short shots o' rye," drawled Stretch, hooking a heel on the brass rail.

"And a little information," said Larry, glancing about him. "Sheriff Holbrook or the mayor been here?"

"No," said the barkeep, as he began pouring.

Without raising his eyes from his cards, the proprietor, Leo Sharney, explained Mayor Archand was not one of his regulars.

"Favors a higher class place, the mayor. Purtell's Palace or the Territory Club on Harper Street."

"'Obliged," said Larry.

Left-handed, he reached for his drink. Simultaneously, he glanced to the mirror behind and above the bar and glimpsed a battered, bruised, vaguely-familiar face. The man slumped at the corner table wasn't sleeping. He had raised his face and his gunhand and his gun was leveled when Larry whirled and emptied his holster. The seated man fired. His bullet sped past Larry's left ear and shattered a bottle on the shelf and, by then, the barkeep had dropped out of sight, the two old timers were huddled under their table and Sharney had flopped to his knees.

Larry's Colt roared while Stretch drew his matched .45's and darted wary glances every whichaway. The impact of Larry's bullet drove his would-be killer out of his chair to crash against the wall and loose a howl of agony.

"Rear door!" gasped Sharney.

Stretch cocked his lefthand Colt and looked to the partly-open door of the rear room. When he squeezed trigger, he could see only the barrel of a six-gun, but that was enough. The man whose face had been clawed by Kate Preston emerged from the room with his gunhand sagging, his legs buckling and his chest bloody.

As Stretch backstepped clear of the bar, Larry crouched and took sight on the open window south side of the barroom. He had a good enough reason. A gun had boomed in the side alley and the slug had come close enough for him to feel its hot wind at his neck. He aimed for the gunflash and, with his Colt booming in his fist, got off three fast ones, cocking and triggering at speed.

"Up!" Sharney called to Stretch.

And, when Stretch raised his eyes, the fourth man was atop the stairs and aiming at him. He sidestepped as he cut loose with both guns. The unfired weapon spun from the killer's hand as he shuddered from the impact of the bullets. Forward he fell, flopping to the stairs and, belly-down, sliding into the barroom, leaving a trail of blood.

"That — that's all of 'em," breathed Sharney.

"Take a look at 'em," Larry ordered Stretch, gesturing to the body below the stairs and the man huddled this side of the rear door. "I'll check the corner and the alley."

He hurried to the corner, kicked the fallen pistol out of reach of the man slumped and groaning there, then dashed to the window. Somebody had fetched a lantern into the alley. By its light, a group of locals gaped at the mortal remains of Larry's second target. He turned away from the window and darted a glance at Stretch, who shrugged and shook his head.

"Done for, runt. Won't beat up on no more widows."

"That makes three," said Larry, jerking a thumb. "The hero in the corner got my slug in his shoulder."

"This town got a deaf sheriff for gosh sakes?" Stretch asked irritably.

"He'll be along," sighed Sharney, trudging to the bar. "Purtell's and the Territory Club — both close enough for him to hear the shooting."

Just as Sharney finished speaking, the sheriff of Bridger County came charging in with gun drawn. Close behind him was a portly, well-groomed man whom Larry assumed to be the mayor. Right now he had eyes only for Breck Holbrook. He had known a great many mean-tempered lawmen in his time, but had rarely seen one as angry-eyed, as grim-visaged as this grey-suited, black sombreroed keeper of the peace. Holbrook looked to be thirty or thereabouts, a lean six-footer and formidable, braced in the centre of the barroom, brandishing a cocked Colt. Formidable, sure, but mostly furious.

As his gaze fell on the dead men, Mayor Cleaver Archand flinched and said,

"Hell's bells."

Backs to the bar, the Texans ejected their spent shells into spittoons, tugged fresh cartridges from their belts and reloaded. The barkeep was upright and performing again, pouring a sizeable shot for his trembling employer.

"And a stiff one for yourself, Jerry," urged Sharney. "And no short shots for our tall friends. They'll be drinking doubles."

From the alley, old Aaron called to his boss.

"Another'un out here, Breck."

"Dead?" scowled Holbrook.

"With one 'tween his eyes and another in his heart, ain't no way he could be otherwise," came Aaron's cheerful reply.

The Texans holstered their Colts and nodded curtly to the sheriff. Larry gestured to the corner and informed him,

"I think my first slug busted his shoulder."

Dark and moody, Holbrook's eyes flicked from Larry to Stretch. They were drinking now.

"Any other casualties?" he demanded.

"Zeke and Dewey are too old for this kind of excitement," muttered Sharney, glancing to the old timers now picking themselves up. "But another shot of whatever's their pleasure should chase the chill out of their guts."

"All right," said Holbrook, hammering down and holstering his pistol. "Make it short and clear, Sharney. Speeches I don't need."

"Set-up," said Sharney.

"Damn right," growled the barkeep. "It would've been bloody murder — if these strangers wasn't so quick-brained and gun-fast."

"You mind if Jerry tells it?" begged

Sharney, raising his glass again. "I need this."

"Go ahead, Ness," nodded Holbrook.

"They came in about an hour ago," the barkeep told him. "Looked like they'd been wrasslin' mountain lions. Faces bruised — one of 'em scratched up bad. Things were quiet till one of 'em, the one by the front window, looked out and saw somethin'." He gestured to the Texans, "Them, I guess."

His glass half-empty, Sharney winced and recalled,

"All of a sudden their guns were out."

"Swore we'd be the first to get it if any of us tipped their hand," said Jerry Ness. "Then they staked out, one of 'em upstairs, one of 'em in the back room, one in the alley and him in the corner."

"These gents arrived and — I don't know when they got wise," muttered Sharney, his eyes on Larry.

"You and the barkeep and the old

fellers — all plenty nervous," drawled Larry. "That's what made us leery. Then I looked in the mirror and recognized the hombre in the corner, he was drawin' a bead, so . . . "

"So we just naturally defended ourselves," shrugged Stretch.

"You say you recognized one of them?" Holbrook challenged Larry.

"Him first," said Larry, nodding to the corner. "Then the others made their play."

"Same four sonsabitches," growled Stretch.

"Who were they, and where . . . ?" began Holbrook.

"Tell you all about it," said Larry. "In your office."

"I wanted to warn you rightaway," frowned Sharney. "But they swore — if we tried anything . . . "

"You did fine by us," Larry assured him.

"And we're obliged," said Stretch.

At that point, old Aaron came ambling in to report the body in the alley was now en route to the funeral parlor.

"Have the other two taken out of here," ordered Holbrook. "I want the contents of their pockets, all items of identification, on my desk within the quarter-hour."

"You just leave that to me, Breck," grinned Aaron. "How about the loser with the busted shoulder? Take him to Maurie Edwards?"

"Put him in a cell," scowled Holbrook. "Doc Edwards can tend him there." As the deputy retreated to the batwings to summon help, the sheriff remarked to the mayor, "Our discussion will have to be postponed. Thanks for the hospitality and your good intentions, Mayor Archand, but, as you can see, I'm back on duty now."

"Yes, of course." After a curious glance at the Texans, Archand turned to leave. "Well, you know where to find me, Sheriff. To you, my door is always open."

"Yours," Holbrook said bitterly. "But

how many others?"

After the mayor's departure, the Texans drained their glasses. Larry dropped money on the bar, accorded Sharney and Ness a friendly nod and followed Holbrook from the saloon with Stretch tagging. There was no conversation before they reached the law office.

Without waiting for an invitation, they helped themselves to chairs and fished out their makings. Holbrook seated himself at his desk, tossed his hat to a peg and lit a cigar. He was ready to question them, but now the wounded, unconscious survivor of that bloody affray was carried in to be installed in the cell block under Aaron's supervision and the doctor was arriving. During this, Larry kept an eye on Holbrook, studying the handsome face covertly, reading the signs of tension, resentment and grim resignation. Plainly, the county sheriff was one mighty discontented lawman.

As Aaron followed the stretcher-bearers out, he assured his boss,

"I'll be back from the funeral parlor purty soon."

He closed the street-door behind him. Holbrook worked his cigar to the left side of his mouth and eyed the strangers impatiently.

"I'm waiting for an explanation. And I'll thank you to identify yourselves."

"He's Emerson, I'm Valentine," said Larry.

"Three men dead and one wounded because they tried to kill you," said Holbrook. "What was their motive?"

"I guess they hankered to pay us off," shrugged Larry.

"We had a run-in with 'em this afternoon," drawled Stretch. "Time we were through with 'em they were hurtin'."

"But then we forgot about 'em," said Larry. "Didn't figure on ever seein' 'em again."

"That's all there is to it?" challenged Holbrook. He scowled irritably. "You

60

could've told me this at Sharney's."

"No," said Larry. "There was a lady involved, so I'm tellin' you private. You don't talk of such things in a saloon."

"Wouldn't seem fair to the lady," explained Stretch.

"Southern chivalry," said Holbrook, with an impatient shrug. "All right, let's hear the whole story."

In terse sentences, Larry reported their encounter with runty Jarvis Preston, their visit to the Wolf Creek spread and the violent action that followed. Then, while Holbrook glowered indignantly, he went on to air his views on the subject of the widow's plight, the indignities she had to endure, the unwelcome attentions of Council Valley cowhands who considered her fair game. He finished off with a few scathing remarks about the indifference of the county law and, by then, Holbrook was florid with fury; Stretch half-expected he would rise and hurl himself at Larry.

He pounded the desk-top. Sparks

flew from his cigar as he raged at them.

"You damn heroes dare to accuse me of — of ignoring that kind of situation? What do I know of the Preston woman? Practically nothing! She has a reputation for behaving rashly any time a rider comes by — and for her hair-trigger temper. The Wild Widow, they call her. If ranch-hands have been trespasssing, harassing her, why hasn't she filed a formal complaint? That's what I'm here for."

"You'd go against them big-shot ranchers of the valley?" Larry asked dubiously. "Kick a few butts, use your manacles, throw a few cowhands in jail?"

"I serve the whole county and every citizen," declared Holbrook. "Town-folk, cattlemen, homesteaders, anybody living within the boundaries of Bridger County. I don't play favorites and you can bet your Texas spurs I don't tip my hat to the Kipps, the McCords or any other ranchers — no matter how wealthy they are. In my bailiwick, no man is above the law."

"So maybe we pegged you wrong," Larry conceded, matching stares with Holbrook.

"I get that impression," retorted Holbrook. "And now I'm asking what brings you hot-shots to Cormack? Quite an entrance you've made. First the ruckus at Wolf Creek, then a barroom gunfight with three dead and one wounded. You look like ranch-hands but operate like free-riding vigilantes." Cold-eyed, he added, "And I don't like that."

The taller Texan slumped lower in his chair and suddenly became interested in the fly-specked ceiling. Larry dribbled smoke through his nostrils, squinted warily into Holbrook's truculent visage and assured him,

"There are things *we* don't like. Such as trail-trash gangin' up on a lone woman. Such as killers settin' us up."

"Things like that . . . " Stretch

63

shrugged casually. "We get kinda irritated."

"We didn't come to this territory for any special reason," said Larry. "Now that we're here, we'll side the widow a while. And this you better believe. We'll be somethin' better'n hired hands. While we're at Wolf Creek, we'll be her bodyguards."

"Which means any skirt-chasin' skunk comes sniffin' around her . . . " began Stretch.

"Is gonna wish he was someplace else," finished Larry. "So now you know where we stand."

"You work for a rancher, you have to be ready for any kind of trouble, I'll grant you that," muttered Holbrook. "But don't leave yourselves open for charges — such as assault. If you have to get rough, be damn sure the trespasser makes the first aggressive move." He gestured brusquely. "That's all. You can go now."

Stretch darted a quick glance at his partner, fearing the worst. But, to his relief, Larry appeared cold-calm as they got to their feet. They walked out of Holbrook's office while, two miles north of the Bridger County border, the most dangerous predator ever to enter this region squatted by a campfire, stared into the gathering dusk and predicted to his companion,

"Within a few days of my reaching Cormack, a fine citizen of that town will be ruined and wishing he'd never been born."

3

Background of a Badge-Toter

THE speaker was Garth Norman, a lean rogue whose rusty black suit and flat-brimmed hat gave him the look of an itinerant preacher. His gleaming eyes were dark, his complexion sallow, but not much of it visible. For his purposes he had stopped shaving many months before; now the mustache was thick and flowing, the bushy beard hanging to his chest. He was armed, but his pistol was well-concealed.

"You're some hater, friend, I'll say that for you," the other man cheerfully remarked. "Got a real heavy chip on your shoulder, huh?"

"I could kill him easily enough," muttered Norman. "But death would be too merciful. It's important to me that he suffers, that his spirit is broken, that he ends up losing everything."

"I don't reckon I'd enjoy to be in his shoes," grinned the cheerful one.

Calvin Fulbright was, at this time, posing as a peddler. They were camped by a trail leading south into Bridger County, the four team-animals and Norman's saddler picketed and feeding a few yards from the gaily-painted wagon. Red lettering on the canopy proclaimed its owner to be C. Fulbright, Esquire, whose 'traveling emporium' carried wares of every kind. For a vital reason, the wagon was positioned a respectful distance from the fire. Of chunky physique, Fulbright was blond and dapper, affecting a checkered suit, tan derby and fancy vest and cravat. Like Norman, he wore his handgun shoulder-holstered.

"I'll move on after breakfast," said Norman. "You know what you have to do. Give me a couple of hours start. After you arrive, we'll pretend to become acquainted, just as though we've met for the first time."

"Your back-up will be there by now," guessed Fulbright.

"They won't be hard to find," shrugged Norman. "Any saloon."

"Reliable, you said," drawled Fulbright, prodding at their slow-frying supper.

"Reliable enough," said Norman. "For what they have to do, they don't need to be in the genius class."

"Yeah, sure, but remember now," offered Fulbright. "If they've let you down, if you just can't find them in Cormack, you won't have to give up on our little plan. I'm confident I can provide five trusty substitutes inside a couple of days. You'll recall I spoke of them before. The Emhardt brothers and their three sidekicks."

"Garrett wouldn't dare fail me," Norman coldly assured him. "He'll be there — waiting."

"Five years in a territorial prison sure changes a man," remarked Fulbright, studying him intently. "I remember how you were when they sent you away. Uncouth is the word that comes to my mind. No offense, Garth. You looked hard case and talked hard case."

"I've had five years of waiting and planning," scowled Norman. "And plenty of time to improve my speech. It can be mighty useful, learning to speak as an educated man. It helped kill time and I had a good teacher. In fact, that's what he used to be before he found his wife with another man and knifed them both. We called him Professor. He'll die in that stinking hell-hole, but I'm out. I served my term and I'm out and free to even my score."

"Didn't take you long to get yourself a good horse, new duds and a bankroll." Fulbright chuckled callously. "How many dead did it take?"

"Just a couple," shrugged Norman. "And you? Are you telling me you worked for wages to pay for the rig and stock it with merchandise?"

Fulbright, as cold-blooded and homicidal as Norman, grinned and winked and assured him.

"I didn't leave any live witnesses. Not my style."

Conversation ceased for a while. Norman brooded in silence until Fulbright had dished up and they were satisfying their appetites. He then insisted Fulbright repeat certain information.

"Again?" grinned Fulbright.

"I want to hear it again — because it pleases me," Norman said stony-faced.

"Well, like I told you before, it was just one of those crazy coincidences," said Fulbright. "We met in a bar in Laramie, this insurance salesman and me, and he was in a mood for talking and griping. He's with the Blackhawk company and all caught up in his work. You know the kind. Real hot-shot. The kind who'd bend a sodbuster's ear for an hour or more just to sell him the idea of insuring his chicken-coop or his privy. If it was up to him, every citizen would insure every damn thing. Not just his life, but everything he owns."

"And he'd been working Cormack

just a week before," mused Norman.

"Right," nodded Fulbright. "And he tried his pitch on Penn."

"And Penn . . . " In his unholy glee, Norman almost gagged on a half-chewed mouthful. "Penn wasn't buying."

"Don't believe in insurance, Penn said," chuckled Fulbright. "Life, property or anything else. He's just not worrying about his future, has all the security any man needs. Business is good and his savings are safe in the Meldrum Reliance Bank."

"You're dead sure about . . . ?" began Norman.

"Dead sure," declared Fulbright. "With the founder and manager of the Reliance Bank, the Blackhawk man failed again. Seems Mister Chester Meldrum and his friend Penn share the same opinion of the insurance business."

Norman's bearded visage was blank, only his moody eyes showing expression, as he predicted.

"They'll feel differently about the benefits of insurance, and very soon. But, by then, it'll be too late. Especially for Penn."

"Every time you say his name, it's as if you're spitting," observed Fulbright.

"After we're through in Cormack," muttered Norman, "I'll spit him out of my mind forever. I'll forget him — never think of him again."

★ ★ ★

For the trouble-shooters, supper had gotten lost in the shuffle. But, hungry though they were, they stabled their horses and checked into a hotel before investigating the eating houses of Cormack.

Being comfortably solvent — on their standards — they toted their saddlebags, packrolls and sheathed Winchesters into the lobby of the town's finest hotel, the tripe-storied Penn House on North Main Street, there to be accorded a somewhat restrained welcome. Obviously the Penn House catered to a high-class type of transient, and these tall strangers looked to be little better than trail-bums. To his credit, the night-clerk was discreet.

"By the day or by the week?" he courteously enquired, inking a pen and offering it to Larry.

"Just for tonight," Larry said gruffly. He signed the register and passed the pen to his partner. "We're payin' in advance and, listen, mister, do yourself a kindness and quit your frettin'."

"You don't need to worry about us," drawled Stretch, after scrawling his name. "Pure truth is we're plumb respectable. But we got this old problem . . . "

"Meanin' we know what we look like," nodded Larry.

"And we can guess what you're thinkin'," said Stretch.

"Well . . . " began the clerk.

"Don't worry about it," soothed Larry. "You got our word we ain't about to ride our horses into your fancy dinin' room nor spit on your floor nor cuss in front of the ladies."

"Won't scratch up the bed-linen neither," promised Stretch. "Always take off our spurs before we turn in." He grinned his guileless grin. "Our boots too."

"I believe you," chuckled the clerk. "Ground floor double suit you?"

"That'll do fine," said Larry.

"Number Six just along the corridor," said the clerk, taking a key from the rack. He made change from the bill proffered by Larry and nodded affably. "Hope you'll be comfortable, gents."

It took the Texans only a few moments to stow their gear in Number 6 along the corridor. They then returned to the lobby to question the clerk.

"I crave Chinese cookin'," explained Stretch. "Chow mein, you know? Maybe chop suey. Maybe a couple dishes of both."

"Tell me Cormack's got no Chinese hash-house and you're gonna break my partner's heart," drawled Larry.

"Canton Cafe just around the corner," offered the clerk.

"*Muchas gracias*," grunted Stretch.

Soon afterward, comfortably settled at a table for two and working their way through heaping helpings of chop suey, the tall men discussed the surliest lawman they had encountered in many a moon. Stretch, always in good humor while satisfying the inner Emerson, remarked the plight of defenseless Kate was no reflection on the county sheriff's attitude toward local rowdies. Breck Holbrook had not been neglectful of his duties. Cantankerous Kate just hadn't thought to appeal for his help.

"Uh huh, sure," nodded Larry, forking up another mouthful. "So I ain't curious any more — about that."

Stretch munched, swallowed and frowned apprehensively.

"Here we go again," he complained. "You ain't curious any more, you said. About that, you said. Meanin' there's another doggone mystery on your mind? Hell sakes, runt, can't you never let up?"

"Where's the harm?" shrugged Larry. "I come up against somethin' I can't savvy, so I get to wonderin' about it. That's natural. Where's the harm?"

"And just what . . . ?" began Stretch.

"Got to be a reason," Larry said calmly.

"For . . . ?" prodded Stretch.

"For the way Holbrook acts," said Larry. "His temper on a short fuse all the time. Some kind of misery's plaguin' that badge-toter, bedevelin' him, sourin' him, and I'm curious is all."

In desperation, Stretch pointed out, "Whatever makes Holbrook so ornery, so mean-tempered, ain't none of your cotton-pickin' business."

Larry eyed him impassively.

"Did I say it was?"

"Well, no," winced Stretch. "But — aw, hell, you're gettin' me all mixed up again."

"Eat your supper," said Larry.

"I'm eatin'," sighed Stretch. "I'm eatin'."

He saved his next question until they had finished their meal, paid their tab and were quitting the cafe. Just how was Mr. Nosey Valentine going to satisfy his curiosity anyway?

"Have to talk to somebody who knows him, I guess," drawled Larry.

"Pardon me for remindin' you," Stretch said in exasperation. "We only just got here. We don't know any of the sheriff's friends. And another thing. He's so ornery it ain't likely he's got any friends anyway."

"Don't have to be a friend," said Larry. "Just somebody who knows him close and maybe understands what's eatin' at him." He sighted a prospect when they reached the main street; they were just in time to spot a familiar figure entering a saloon. "Old Aaron, for instance."

"Yup, maybe so," shrugged Stretch. "Well, he's sociable, come to think of it. Gabby too."

Hurrying along to the saloon of Aaron Dubb's choice, they intercepted the army scout-turned-deputy at the bar, paid for his drink, ordered two of the same and insisted he join them at a corner table. Aaron was agreeable and guessing they were curious, but not about his boss.

He confided that the dead hard cases would be buried tomorrow in an unidentified condition, the wounded prisoner having refused to state his own name, also the names of his cronies.

"Wasn't nothin' in their saddlebags neither. And they were totin' scarce enough dinero to keep 'em eatin'. So what can Breck do but hold our prisoner, him with the busted shoulder, till Circuit-Judge Cooney comes by? Won't matter then. He'll be shipped off to a territorial hoosegow, betcha life. Won't need a name anyway. They'll give him a number and that'll do."

"You enjoyin' the life, Aaron?" asked Larry. "Bein' a deputy?"

"You're lookin' at an uncomplainin' man," grinned Aaron. "Cormack suits me fine. Been deputy here for three years."

"With Sheriff Holbrook all the time?" frowned Larry.

"Nope," grunted Aaron. "Started off with the old sheriff. Martinson was his name. Good man he was, but gettin' too old for the job. Horse threw him. He fell real hard, broke his neck. That was — lemme prod my memory now — uh huh — that'd be four months better'n a year ago."

"So then the town council offered the badge to Holbrook," guessed Stretch.

"Not rightaway," said Aaron. "First they had to send for him. Breck wasn't here. Shucks no. He was up north in a town called Degan City and buildin' hisself quite a reputation, by damn . . . "

The old man talked on, swigged whiskey and talked some more, happy in the company of a couple of good listeners. Thus, the Texans learned something of Breck Holbrook's background. He was by no means a veteran lawman. In Degan City, he was a cashier at the First National Bank and a popular figure with an assured future, but admired more for his gun-skill than for his genial personality; his accuracy with a handgun had become legendary in Degan County. As well as carrying off the big prize at Fourth of July shooting contests, young Breck had notched up a score of four dead and four wounded bank bandits. During a one-year period of his employment at the First National, that bank had twice been invaded by hold-up artists. On both occasions, the young teller had whipped out the pistol he still owned, had taken his chances against hardened desperadoes and had inflicted heavy punishment.

Predictably, the editor of the Degan County 'Messenger' had made capital of these incidents and Holbrook's fame had spread.

"Cleave Archand knew all about

him," Aaron told the Texans. "Well, shucks, them Degan newspapers, you'll find 'em all over the territory. So, when Mike Martinson cashed in his chips, the mayor up and told his aldermen pals as how he knew just the right feller to be our new sheriff. They voted on it and they telegraphed Breck and made him an offer and, ever since, we've had us one real smart sheriff, I hope to tell you. Ain't no Council Valley smart-aleck'd dare buck Breck. Some of 'em tried it after he got swore in. And, by damn, Breck had his hogleg out and cocked and coverin' 'em 'fore they could clear leather."

Larry stood another round. The congenial atmosphere was prevailing, so he didn't hesitate to switch the emphasis from the Holbrook prowess to the Holbrook personality.

"So Cormack got a right fine sheriff," he remarked. "That's good for Cormack, but I guess Holbrook's still tryin' to get the hang of sheriffin'.

Been a lawman only a year and four months. So he's still learnin'. Likely frets about it, and that's what makes him so damn miserable."

"Noticed that, did you?" prodded Aaron, frowning at Larry over the top of his glass.

"It shows, old timer," muttered Stretch. "He has sure as hell got a misery chewin' at him."

With a blue-veined hand, Aaron signaled them to lean closer.

"I can tell you 'bout that," he offered. "On accounta he told me. Only he didn't make it a secret, you know? We just got to talkin' one night. It was last month, as I recall. Well, most of what he told me I already guessed. You get to be as old as me, you just nachrally savvy these things."

Not only was Aaron Dubb a shrewd observer of the human condition; there was little he didn't know of the local scene, of the mores and manners of county folk, the well-to-do, the lowly and the in-betweens. Yes, as well as understanding Breck Holbrook, this old timer understood Cormack. The town had made the transition from rowdy trail-camp to well-established Community and Aaron accurately read the signs of its new-won respectability. There was class-consciousness here, and Breck Holbrook had come up against attitudes encountered by many a lawman before him.

"What you have to savvy is, back in Deban City, he was the popular young buck worked at the bank," said Aaron. "Sure, he was good with a six-gun, but that wasn't his regular trade. A bankin' man he was. Plumb respectable. Courtin' a fine lady too. His boss' daughter."

"She turned him down after he accepted Mayor Archand's offer?" asked Larry.

"You guessed it," nodded Aaron. "Married up with some other young feller. Seems she never did take kindly to Breck bein' so handy with a hogleg.

So he came to Cormack to make a new start and — well now — things didn't work out like he expected. Plain truth is he don't like totin' a badge. He's good at the job, gettin' better all the time, but it don't pleasure him none. He can't make no real friends here, he says. Back in Degan, folks was always invitin' him to their homes. But the righteous citizens of this here town'd just as soon he keeps his distance. To them, he's a gunfighter with a badge, just right for sheriff . . . "

"But not the kind of hombre they'll socialize with," guessed Larry. He glanced at his partner. "Sounds familiar."

"Ain't that the truth," muttered Stretch.

"Cleave Archand does his damndest to make Breck feel like he belongs," said Aaron. "I think he genuine likes Breck. Hell of it is, Cleave's high-falutin' wife won't hear no talk of him invitin' Breck to their home. I swear Jessie Archand's as snooty as

Albertina Penn. Jessie bein' the mayor's wife and Albertina's man ownin' the best hotel in town, they figure that makes 'em the boss-hens of the whole county." He shrugged philosophically. "All them righteous folks lookin' down their noses at Breck. What we got here is a real bluenose town, and that's a fact. Cowpokes raise a little hell on paydays, but Breck and me, we keep 'em in line. You'd think they'd appreciate all Breck does for 'em, huh? Our high-class citizens?"

"He gets paid from county funds," mused Larry. "They figure that's enough."

"It ain't that he craves for 'em to pat his back or make speeches at him," said Aaron. "I think he'd settle for 'Howdy, Sheriff. Nice day, Sheriff and how've you been?' But they don't give him even that much. He shows up at the chapel Sundays, they pretend like they don't see him." He thought to assure them, "It don't just make him miserable and lonesome. It makes him good and mad, sore as a new boil."

"Thanks for tellin' us, Aaron," said Larry.

"Yeah, well, just 'tween us, huh?" begged Aaron. "It wasn't no secret, like I said, but I'd as soon Breck didn't know you heard it all from me."

"We won't talk it around," promised Stretch. He slanted a glance at his partner. "Runt, anything else you're curious about?"

"Well . . . " Larry frowned at the deputy, "I got to admit there's somethin' else I don't savvy. It's a big town and I guess Bridger County's a sizeable hunk of territory — so how come Holbrook rates only one sidekick? Council too cheap to pay another deputy?"

"You said it true, friend," nodded Aaron. "The mayor stays after 'em, but them councilmen-tightwads keep sayin' as how one deputy's enough for a hot-shot sheriff with a big reputation." He fished out a timepiece of ancient manufacture and squinted at it. "I best be hittin' the hay now, boys. Thanks for the cheer. Sure appreciate it."

"Our pleasure, old timer," Stretch assured him, as he rose to leave.

"Take care, Aaron," said Larry.

"So that's that," said Stretch, after the old man had left them. "You just had to know, so what d'you say? You satisfied now?"

"Uh huh," grunted Larry. "I won't be wonderin' about Holbrook no more. He wants to act sore . . . " He grimaced resentfully, "I guess he's got good reason."

"We've known a few others like Holbrook," Stretch reminded him. "Save our lives, the good folks say. Keep our town safe for the women and kids. That's what we're payin' you for. But don't be thinkin' we'd want you inside of our homes."

"Holbrook is a hired gun with a badge," nodded Larry. "In his shoes, I'd be feelin' just as ornery."

"You want to talk about the widow-woman now?" asked Stretch. "We gonna hang around Wolf Creek a spell — seein' as how we got nothin' better to do?"

"That's what we'll do," said Larry, finishing his drink. "Check out of the hotel early, grab us some breakfast and head on out to the spread."

Around 10 o'clock that night, when she was about to retire, Kate Preston heard the voices hailing her, baiting her, from the darkness away east of the ranch-house. At least two trespassers, Council Valley riders no doubt, were amusing themselves at her expense. It had happened before and far too often. Yelling protests — plus a great deal of unladylike abuse — had proved futile. Yes, it had happened before and she'd had her fill of it, had even tried to faze them off with her late husband's Winchester.

Furiously, she donned robe and slippers, opened her bedroom window and called her protest.

"Don't you bunkhouse heroes know any better than to pester folks at this hour?"

"Hey, lady, you got a couple admirers out here!" came the mocking reply.

"You feelin' lonesome, ma'am?" the second man taunted her. "Been a long time, huh?"

"All this hollering will wake my children!" she raged.

"So invite us to visit — then we won't have to holler! How about a little company? You're too young a widow to never have no men — and we're sure available!"

The suggestive offers continued while, trembling with indignation, well aware her children were awake and calling to her, she dashed to a closet, opened it and reached for the rifle. She checked its loading, returned to the window and screamed a challenge.

"Last warning! Get off my land — right *now* — or I'll start shooting!"

"Hey *now* we got *trouble*!" a man yelled in mock alarm. "Eagle-Eye

89

Kate — trigger-happy again!"

"We're done for!" guffawed his companion. "Hey, lady, I tell you what! 'Stead of shootin' at us, why don't you invite us over to the house? Then you can look us over and decide who's gonna be the lucky man gets to stay all night with you!"

In blind rage, she leveled the rifle toward the distant voices and began firing, working the lever rapidly. Four shots she triggered. Raucous laughter rose over the din of the first three reports, but then, after the fourth shot, she heard the howl of pain and felt a chill up her spine. There were no more taunts. Moments later, she heard hoofbeats receding eastward.

"Back to bed, you kids!" she gasped, turning from the window.

Tousle-haired and big-eyed, they surveyed her from her bedroom doorway, Irma looking too fretful, too understanding for one so young, Jarvis eagerly enquiring.

"Didja shoot 'em, Ma? Didja?"

She strove to control her trembling as she returned the rifle to the closet.

"Back to your beds *this instant!*" she breathed.

"We're sorry, Mama," murmured her daughter. "And it's awful unfair — the trouble they give you."

"We'll say no more of it," frowned Kate. "Now scat!"

Irma and her brother retreated. Kate sighed worriedly, killed her lamp and stepped out of her slippers, removed her robe and tossed it on the bed. In the gloom, she stared morosely to the left side of the bed.

"I'll have to do it *some* way," she warned herself. "There just has to be another Wolf Creek boss to sleep on that side and be ready to protect us all. Doesn't matter if he's homely or scrawny or fat, just so long as he's willing, just so long as he's my lawful wedded husband."

It was after 11.30 p.m. when the two riders halted their mounts in the broad yard fronting the impressive, double-storied Diamond 7 ranch-house. Moments later, roused from sleep by the excited yells of his bunkhouse gang, the ranch-boss quit his bed, pulled on his boots, ordered his half-awake spouse to stay put and barged forth to investigate the commotion.

On the wrong side of 50, paunchy and irascible Mat McCord invariably rose from his bed on that same side. He was a shade under six feet tall, balding, bulky and bellicose, short on temper and long on autocratic aspirations; to his way of thinking, he was virtual monarch of Diamond 7 and, when he chose to visit the county seat, considered its citizens to be little more than his subjects.

Confused arguments bedevilled his ears as he emerged from the main building to advance on the bunkhouse, a structure double the size of the Diamond 7 barn.

"Oughta have somebody ride in for the doc!"

"Hell with it! He don't need no doc! Hambone'll patch him good enough!"

"Old Mat's gonna raise hell! He'll say we should fetch the doc!"

"If the chuck-boss could fix old Mat's busted rib last winter, he can sure tend Wes."

"Wes . . . ?" roared McCord. No man dared grin at the sight of him, looming in the bunkhouse entrance in nightshirt and boots, his surviving hairs sticking out like straws. "What in blue blazes happened to my son?" He shouldered his way to the table where Wesley Mathew McCord lay stripped to the waist, groaning while chuck-boss Hambone Henshaw swabbed the bullet-gash under his left armpit. "Dammit it t'hell! He's been shot!"

"Bad crease, but he'll mend." This comforting remark was drawled by a nuggety, barrel-chested man with cropped grey hair. Burch Denham by name. Five years his boss' junior, Denham was the Diamond 7 foreman. "I took a good look at it, Mat. He's

93

hurtin', but it could've been a sight worse."

"I want to know who'd dare!" boomed McCord. "What sneakin' lowdown coyote in this whole territory'd *dare* take a shot at *my son*!"

"It was the wild widow-woman, Pa," complained the patient.

"*What* . . . ?" gasped McCord, starting convulsively. "That damn hell-cat . . . ?"

"We were — uh — ridin' home from town, Curly and me," mumbled his pride and joy. "Comin' by the Wolf Creek spread, we just — uh — hollered goodnight — real polite-like. And, next thing we knew, she was blastin' at us from a window." He twisted to catch the eye of the hired hand who brought him home. "Ain't that how it was, Curly?"

Curly Bailes, runty and self-conscious, youngest hand on the Diamond 7 payroll, nodded nervously and kept his gaze averted.

"Well?" challenged McCord. "Cat

got your tongue?"

"Uh — that's how it was, Mister McCord sir," shrugged Curly. "Just how Wes told it."

"She don't get away with *this*!" stormed McCord. "This time, she's gone *too far*! She's gonna rue this night, or my name ain't Mathew McCord!" He whirled to glower at his ramrod. "Burch!"

"Right here beside you," muttered Denham. "You don't have to bull-roar at me."

"Tomorrow mornin', we settle her hash once and for all!" declared McCord. "I want six men mounted and ready to ride right after breakfast! You hear?"

"From the north end of the valley I could hear you," the ramrod said reproachfully.

"Me, you and six good men," snapped McCord. "We're ridin' to Wolf Creek and, by the time I get through bendin' her ear, that fool female'll wish her man had built his spread a million miles from Bridger County! I aim to buy her out or scare her out. Either way. Up to her. This territory ain't big enough for the both of us — meanin' me and any crazy widow-woman who'd shoot my son!"

"You boys sure it happened like you say?" Denham frowned at the patient, then at Curly Bailes. "Exactly like you say?"

"Burch Denham!" gasped McCord. "Am I hearin' you right? Are you darin' to doubt the word of a McCord?"

"Just tryin' to make sense of what they said," shrugged Denham. "Last time I howdied Widow Preston, she sure didn't shoot me. Didn't even pull a gun." On an afterthought, he remarked, "Don't even know if she was packin' a gun. With women, you can't always tell."

"I done gave my orders!" fumed McCord.

"You sure did," sighed Denham. "In spades."

After the treatment of his wound,

the apple of Mat McCord's eye was fed a stiff shot of whiskey and carried to his bedroom in the family home. For the second time that night, the lamps of Diamond 7 were snuffed out. Burch Denham could now retire again to woo sleep, but also to wonder what tomorrow night might bring. It was a small miracle that this veteran cattleman had held his job for so many years.

Unlike his boss, Burch Denham was a reasonable man.

For almost twenty minutes he tossed and turned. And then, always the realist, he accepted the hard fact. There would be no sleep for him this night unless he first alerted a certain party to the possibility of rash action at Wolf Creek.

When needs be, the Diamond 7 ramrod could move as quietly as a marauding redskin. Nobody heard him quit his bunk, don his clothes and leave the bunkhouse. Nobody heard him ride away from the ranch a short time later.

4

Hot Tempers and Cold Nerves

IN the hour after midnight, when the Diamond 7 foreman rode into Cormack, the law office was locked and in darkness. Deputy Aaron Dubb had retired to his usual roost, a bunk in Cell Number 2, the office and jail having become his Cormack home. Sheriff Holbrook's abode was a second floor rear room at the Gilmeyer Hotel on the corner of Main and Goddard.

Without disturbing the snoring night-clerk, Burch Denham checked the register, ascertained the number of the sheriff's room and found his way up there. He rapped gently but persistently until the boss-lawman came awake, lit his lamp and admitted him.

Disgruntled, Holbrook squatted on his bed and surveyed his visitor.

"I'm no liar," he sighed, knuckling at his eyes. "So I don't claim I never forget a name or a face."

"Burch Denham," offered the ramrod. "From Diamond 7? We've talked a couple times. Mostly at the Silver Buckle Saloon on paydays."

"Yes, now I remember you," nodded Holbrook. He checked his watch and grimaced. "You had to wake me — at this hour?"

"When I tell you why, you'll say I did right," Denham assured him. Drawing the room's only chair close to the bed, he proceeded to report recent events and their aftermath, the wounding of Wes McCord, the outraged indignation of his hot-headed sire, the proposed confrontation with the widow. "And maybe you can guess why I'm tippin' you off? Whole thing could get out of hand, Sheriff. Better if you show up, show your badge, so Mat and the boys don't do nothin' rash."

"I'm obliged for the information and, of course, I'll be there," frowned

Holbrook. "But, Denham, do you realize what McCord would say if he knew you'd come to me? He'd accuse you of disloyalty to Diamond 7. He might even fire you."

"I don't mind takin' that chance," shrugged Denham, "on account of I'm a moderate."

"You surprise me," said Holbrook.

"I know what you mean." Denham grinned wryly. "You're an educated man. I'm a saddlesore old cowhand that didn't have much schoolin', so you're wonderin' if I savvy that word. Well, it's what Doc Edwards once called me, and he's as educated as you. Sure, a moderate is what I am."

"So, being a moderate, you'd prefer this visit to Wolf Creek should be non-violent," said Holbrook. Stroking his jaw, eyeing the ramrod intently, he recalled, "You once mentioned McCord's wife, indicating your high regard for the lady. Is it also for her sake you want to forestall McCord's taking the law into his own hands?"

"I ain't no greenhorn hired hand that's stuck on the boss' wife," muttered Denham. "I'm thankful to her is all. About six years ago, when I was laid up with some kind of fever, I don't forget it was Emmie McCord tended me, spoon-fed me, helped Doc Edwards pull me through."

"An excellent reason," Holbrook commented.

"I got another," said Denham.

"Which is?" prodded Holbrook.

"I can't guarantee they're lyin', young Wes and his buddy," said Denham, "but I don't believe the widow got to shootin' for no reason. Wes is spoiled and too sassy for his own good and his buddy Curly is just a tagalong, know what I mean?"

"In other words, the other boy may know more than he's telling," guessed Holbrook. "All right, I'll remember that. Might just have a little private parley with — what's his name?"

"Bailes," said Denham. "I don't

know his given handle. We all call him Curly."

"Thanks for letting me know," said Holbrook, stifling a yawn. "If there's nothing else, you'd better return to Diamond 7 and get some sleep — and I'll do likewise."

As he rose to leave, Denham pointed out,

"Mat won't be expectin' to see you at Wolf Creek. You — uh — won't let on . . . ?"

"He'll never know we had this little conference," Holbrook assured him. "I could claim I'm there on official business anyway. You probably haven't heard. The lady was assaulted by marauders today."

"What . . . ?" began Denham.

"They weren't Council Valley men," shrugged Holbrook. "Four strangers. Fortunately for Mrs Preston, two other strangers happened by at the crucial moment and sent them running."

"Life is sure rough for widows," remarked Denham, opening the door.

"I wouldn't know," said Holbrook. "I'm not personally acquainted with any widows."

* * *

It was early, less than ten minutes after sunrise, when the Texans tied their horses to the rail in front of a small cafe, Barney's Place. Intrigued that any Cormack hash-house should be open quite this early, but grateful too, they ventured inside to savor the appetising aromas wafting from the kitchen. The proprietor, flabby and bleary-eyed, came to the kitchen entrance to squint at them.

"We too early for breakfast?" asked Larry.

"You're sure early," said Barney. "But not too early. Just give me a few minutes to dish up."

He was as good as his word. Only a few minutes later, occupying the table nearest the kitchen, their taste-buds rampant, they reacted happily to his setting laden platters before them.

"I'm always up early," he volunteered as they began eating. "It's all the worry, you see. Not a full night's sleep have I had since my wife up and left me. Went home to her mother in Culbertsburg, Nebraska. And now I can't sleep for worryin' about her."

"That's plumb sad," Stretch sympathized.

"Worry, worry, worry," sighed Barney.

"Culbertsburg, Nebraska," Larry mused with his mouth full. "That a quiet town, law-abidin' and all?"

"Oh, sure," shrugged Barney.

"Well, I don't know as you have to worry," offered Larry. "She's likely safe enough there."

The cafe-owner eyed him blankly before returning to his kitchen.

"*That's* not what I'm worryin' about," he growled. "What worries me is maybe she'll forgive me and come back to me!"

Some short time later, having accounted for a formidable quantity of ham, eggs, hot biscuits and coffee, the troubleshooters decided they were ready for their journey to Wolf Creek and a morning of flushing Preston strays out of the brush and timber and back to home range. They paid for their breakfast, wished the proprietor an indefinite separation from his spouse and set forth.

Because his sleep had been interrupted, Cormack's sheriff roused from slumber an hour later than usual. This irritated him and, while bathing and shaving he brooded again on the hand dealt him by fickle Fate. Nowadays, he was too easily irritated.

"Not the man you used to be," he reflected while plying his razor. "Too many wrong decisions you've made, hot-shot, and now you're paying for them. Improving yourself, getting a better education, wasn't such a bad idea. But getting into the banking business, getting to be fast with a forty-five, winning a reputation, was a sorry mistake. You should never have resettled in Degan City. Too bad you didn't appreciate what you had in Huron Ford, Dakota."

Self-recrimination didn't help. Venturing forth in search of breakfast, his grim mood prevailed. And, later, when he entered his office, he still wore the expression so familiar to old Aaron.

"Keep an eye on things a while," he urged. "Seems I have to take a morning ride."

"Uh huh." Aaron nodded affably. "Where you headed?"

"Wolf Creek," said Holbrook.

"Need some kind of affidavit from the widow-lady, huh?" asked Aaron. "About that deviltry yesterday?"

"I wouldn't want to revive the widow's memory of that incident," frowned Holbrook. "But those Texans claim she's been pestered by Council Valley riders. I think I should hear what she has to say about that."

"Back by noon, I guess" suggested Aaron. "So on your way, Breck boy."

"I've never even met the Preston woman," grouched Holbrook. "You'd better tell me any short-cut you know of — to Wolf Creek. Then I'll be on my way."

When the Texans rode into the yard, Irma was emerging from the ranch-house to join the Kipp children on their mare. Jarvis came scuttling out to accord the tall men a joyful welcome and, her curiosity aroused, Kate moved to the kitchen entrance in time to see Stretch boosting her daughter onto the mare.

"You came back." She worked up a smile. "I'm glad to see you. Does this mean . . . ?"

"Means we'll try educatin' your herd," drawled Larry, doffing his Stetson. "Well, heck. Somebody's got to teach 'em."

"Cattle can be plenty dumb," remarked Stretch. "If I was a Hereford steer, I bet I'd have savvy enough to stay where there's grass for the eatin'. Don't fret about it, ma'am. We'll teach 'em good."

"I'm glad you are not a steer, Mister Emerson," giggled Irma.

"Well," he shrugged, "I guess that makes two of us."

The mare's small riders waved cheerily to Kate and the Texans and made off toward the town-trail. Jarvis then caused his mother some irritation by announcing his intention of riding double with 'Uncle Stretch' and learning how to flush strays. He was fired with the ambition to become a top hand and seemingly oblivious to the obvious drawback, his size, his tender years — all four of them.

Overcoming her irritation, Kate patiently explained her son would have to wait a few years.

"You have to be older, taller and stronger for such chores."

The boy's disappointment was comical, but the Texans didn't laugh.

"There's other chores you can take

care of, amigo," Larry told him. "Real important chores."

"But I want to work with you," pleaded Jarvis.

"I'm talkin' about somethin' you can do for us," declared Larry, as he detached his saddlebags. "We ain't about to hunt strays with our horses totin' all our gear."

"That's right," nodded Stretch. He took his cue from Larry and began unslinging his packroll. "So we need for a good man to take charge of this stuff."

"Reckon you can handle it, ol' buddy?" asked Larry. "You don't have to tote everything at one time. Just bit by bit is okay."

"Where to?" demanded Jarvis.

"Bunkhouse," said Larry.

"And, listen, we're countin' on you to pick us the best bunks and stow our belongin's neat," warned Stretch.

"You don't try to pull the rifles out of the scabbards, understand?" cautioned Larry. "Just tote 'em like they are, keep the packs rolled and the saddlebags closed."

The personal effects of the drifters made a mound beside the corral. Proudly, full of importance now, the boy began the first of his six journeys to the bunkhouse. Watching him trudge away, hefting Stretch's sheathed Winchester, Kate quit the porch. The Texans remounted, waiting for her to join them.

"You know, you have a real feeling for kids, both of you," she told them earnestly. "I swear I'll never understand why you've never married. You have fatherly instincts and you're respectful of women." Arms akimbo, she studied them in genuine astonishment. "Are you *sure* neither of you wants to marry me?"

"She's doin' it again!" fretted Stretch.

"I already warned her, but she acts like she never heard a word I said," complained Larry, frowning down at her. "We're here to help out, Kate. But that's all, understand? Ain't gonna be no courtin', no weddin' bells. Now you go tend your chores and we'll tend ours."

"I only asked you a question," she frowned.

"Some question," said Stretch, shuddering.

They wheeled their mounts and began their scout of Wolf Creek range while, along the town-trail, the lone rider passed the mare toting the Kipp children and Kate's eldest. The intent appraisal of the small fry disquieted Holbrook. He had nothing against children, but was more at ease around adults. Except in Cormack, he reminded himself as he rode on. Cormack, his new hometown wherein the better-class citizenry kept their doors shut against him.

A quarter-mile closer to his destination, he felt his horse falter and at once guessed he would be forced to slow his pace. Shrugging resignedly, he reined up, dismounted and checked the animal's right forehoof.

"Loose shoe." He grimaced in exasperation.

Two nails and a hammer would swiftly remedy this condition. He could handle it himself upon reaching the Preston ranch, he assured himself. But he would have to let the horse choose its own pace; nothing to be gained by hustling the animal under these conditions. He would be delayed. And, if the Diamond 7 men arrived before him . . .

In their first investigation of the brush this side of the creek the Texans extricated five rebellious bunch-quitters and, with much cussing and fazing, hustled them out of there and onto feed-graze. It was then that Stretch chanced to glance northward and spot the dust-cloud moving in from the east.

"Passel of riders movin' on the house," he called to Larry, who promptly put his sorrel to the slope of a rise. Patiently, the taller Texan waited. When Larry rejoined him he asked, "Hostile or friendly — what'd you say?"

"Ask me again when we're lookin' 'em over," muttered Larry. "I counted eight."

"Best we head back," opined Stretch.

"You know it," growled Larry. "Let's go."

By the time they were reining up beside the corral, the heated exchange was well and truly under way. From the porch, with her son clinging to her skirts, Kate angrily denied the accusations hurled at her by the only intruder who had so far dismounted, Mat McCord himself. Dunham and the other men sat their mounts, warily appraising the Texans.

"They were trespassing, Mister McCord!" snapped Kate. "And that's not all . . . !"

"The man you shot — and could've killed — was my boy Wes!" raged McCord. "And, consarn you, woman, he was only takin' a short-cut, him and his buddy!"

"Taking a short-cut and a lot of liberties!" she retorted. "They shouted — insulting remarks. I won't take that kind of talk from your son or any other man!"

"That's a damn-blasted lie!" gasped McCord.

"Easy, Mat," chided Denham.

"You butt out of this!" scowled McCord.

"Uh — hold on now, mister," drawled Larry, fixing the rancher with his eye. "Seems like your temper's workin' faster'n your brain. Slow down a mite."

"Ain't polite, you and the lady hollerin' thisaway," remarked Stretch. "Let's keep it friendly, huh?"

"Who in blazes are these no-accounts?" demanded McCord.

"Only hands I've been able to hire since my man died — if that's any of your business," said Kate.

"Hired hands, huh?" challenged McCord, glaring at the Texans. "And you got the nerve to back-talk *me*?

114

Well, heed this well, consarn you. I'm Mat McCord and I own Diamond 7 and no hired hand sasses me! From hired hands, I get respect — or else!"

"Tell you what, Mister McCord," countered Larry. "If you want respect from us, you better show respect for Mrs Preston."

"On account of," said Stretch, "she's a lady."

At that, a burly Diamond 7 man made a growling sound and bunched a fist.

"Are we gonna let these jaspers talk that way to the boss?" he challenged his cohorts. "Or are we gonna teach 'em a lesson?"

"That's enough, Carney," frowned Denham.

But the burly waddy and two others ignored the ramrod and began walking their animals toward the Texans.

"No — wait — please . . . !" began Kate.

"Don't fret about this, ma'am," Stretch said soothingly. "Ain't gonna be no rough stuff."

"Unless these heroes push their luck," said Larry.

"Call 'em off, Mat," begged Denham. "This is no good."

"The hell it ain't!" scowled McCord. "A good lickin' is just what these smart-alecks're beggin' for! Go get 'em, Carney!"

The man addressed was the first to attack and therefore the first casualty. He charged his mount at Larry's sorrel, swung a big fist and at once came to grief. Larry threw his left up to block the swing and his right to Carney's face. Bloody-nosed and dazed, Carney parted company with his horse hitting the dirt with a dull thud.

One of Carney's buddies mouthed an oath and, moving in on the taller Texan, slid his boots from stirrups and leapt. The impact shoved Stretch off-balance and he went down heavily, his assailant pounding at him, while the third man attempted a similar assault on Larry. He too eased his boots from stirrups. He too vaulted off his horse to hurl himself sideways but, unlike his cohort failed to topple his target. Larry's fast-swinging right checked him in mid-flight, bouncing off his jaw, rendering him unconscious. Like an unstrung puppet, he collapsed between the two animals.

"I wouldn't," Denham warned the other three.

He could have saved his breath. The still-mounted cowpokes were already deciding against imitating the action of their colleagues. Bug-eyed, they watched Stretch dispose of the man who had pulled him down. From the dust rose the taller Texan, his assailant struggling but helpless, grasped by collar of jacket and slack of pants.

"You mind steppin' aside," Stretch politely requested the apoplectic McCord, as he advanced on him with his yelling captive.

The rancher darted clear of the trough between the hitchrail and Kate's flower-patch and, with no apparent effort, Stretch flipped his attacker over the rail. Full-length and face first, the man flopped into the trough and floundered.

"You did that real neat," Larry said approvingly. "I thought sure he'd bust his head on this end of the trough, but no. Real neat, amigo."

"He's kinda moist," observed Stretch. "But better he gets dunked than busts his head."

"Whoo-eee . . . !" cried the enraptured Jarvis.

"You shouldn't be looking," chided his mother.

"Aw, shoot," grinned Jarvis. "*You* looked, Ma."

"What the hell're you waitin' for?" In shock, but in good voice, McCord ranted at Denham and the other men. "You saw what these no-accounts did to Carney and Shoup and Lanahan! Are you gonna let 'em get away with it?"

"They saw, Mat," nodded Denham. He glanced at the gaping horsemen and grinned. "I'd reckon they're thinkin' it over."

The Texans were perched on a toprail of the corral, boredly building cigarettes, McCord still raging at his unscathed employees, one struggling soggily from the trough and two still horizontal, when Breck Holbrook led his limping horse into the yard. He thought to doff his hat to Kate before hurling a reprimand at the rancher.

"Mister McCord, I'll thank you to cease that bellowing!"

"Oh, you will, will you?" snarled McCord, turning to glower at him.

"Take it easy, Mat," muttered Denham. "What can you win by cussin' the sheriff?"

"*I'll* answer that question," offered Holbrook, matching McCord's stare. "Three or four days in the county jail — to cool off."

"Why, you . . . !" began McCord.

"*Enough!*" warned Holbrook. "First and last warning, Mister McCord. Any time you feel like abusing me, make sure I'm not wearing my badge of office." He stepped clear of his horse, glanced about him and frowned irascibly. "All right now, exactly what is happening here?" As McCord turned red and opened his mouth, he raised a hand. "Ladies first, if you please."

"I took a shot at a couple of trespassers last night," said Kate. "Mister McCord tells me one of them was his son and that I near killed him, but . . . " She paused to dismiss her keenly interested son. "Jarvis go inside."

"Aw, Ma . . . " he grouched.

"'Scuse me, ma'am," called Stretch. He lit his cigarette, descended from the rail and ambled to Holbrook's animal. Boy can come with me. Might be we can oblige the sheriff, Jarvis ol' buddy. Seems like this critter near threw a shoe."

"The shack other side of the barn," offered Kate. "Joe and the hands used to do some blacksmithing. I think you'll find what you need."

"Thank you," said Holbrook.

"My pleasure," shrugged Stretch, crooking a finger. "Tag along with me, bub. 'Case I need your help."

Jarvis obediently quit the porch. Stretch took the rein of the lawman's animal and led it away with the boy at his side, thus ensuring he would be out of earshot for the remainder of the confrontation. The battered cowhands revived shakily, picked themselves up and trudged to their horses. Kate then offered her version of last night's intrusion on her privacy and, flushing angrily, repeated some of the remarks voiced by the intruders.

McCord was quick to refute the widow's complaint.

"All Wes and young Curly did was call a polite goodnight — and then this fool female cut loose with a rifle! That's attempted murder, Holbrook! So do your duty!"

"Mrs Preston's word against your son's?" challenged Holbrook.

"Damn right," nodded McCord.

"They're lying!" gasped Kate.

"Leave this to me," Holbrook ordered her. He eyed McCord steadily. "All right now, Mister McCord. If you insist justice is to be done, certain procedures are called for. Upon receipt of your son's written complaint against the lady, I'll obtain a warrant for her arrest and take her into custody."

"Well, get on with it!" scowled McCord.

"Mat, you ought to think twice about . . . " began Denham.

"That's enough out of you, Burch Denham!" snapped McCord.

"Mrs. Preston will be held on a charge of assault with a firearm," Holbrook continued. "She'll be accommodated at the county jail pending the arrival of the circuit-judge. He's not due until the end of next month and, of course, Mrs Preston's children can't be left out here to fend for themselves, so they'll have to accompany her. It'll be awkward. I don't know if the Cormack jail ever accommodated a mother and children before, but I'll just have to make them as comfortable as possible."

"You're tryin' to shame me!" accused McCord.

"I haven't finished," Holbrook said sternly. "Mark this well, Mister McCord. When this case goes to court, your son and his friend will be required to testify under oath. And the county will appoint a defense attorney for the lady. Also, *her* evidence will be heard. Maybe you won't be too embarrassed that a defenseless widow is standing trial for shooting your son, but I wouldn't count on that."

McCord's face was a study. Florid and sweating, plagued by doubt, he shook a fist at Holbrook and announced he would take care of this hell-cat in his own way. What did he need with the law anyway? Jabbing a finger at Kate, he warned,

"You're gonna regret this, I swear. Time I get through talkin' to my neighbors, there won't be a cattleman in this territory who'd raise a hand to help you. If you're smart, you'll sell out and quit Bridger County and never come back!"

"If I ever quit," flared Kate, "it'll be *my* idea! You think a widow can't be independent? Well, guess again, Mister Mean-Mouth McCord! You can't scare me — because you're the *littlest* man I ever knew!"

"Every man's hand'll be against you . . . !" roared McCord.

He was good for another tirade and it might have gone on indefinitely but for Larry's grim interjection. All eyes turned to the Texan on the toprail as he said his piece, not loudly, not with threatening gestures but quietly, compellingly.

"If you plan on turnin' the whole territory against Mrs Preston, you better be sure they know she ain't alone now. And tell 'em what happened here this mornin'."

Before McCord could find his voice again, Holbrook contributed a piece of information that caused the Diamond 7 men to eye Larry warily.

"You may not have heard. Four strangers attacked Mrs Preston yesterday afternoon and, fortunately for her — but not for them — this man and his friend just happened to arrive at that time. I'm holding one of those strangers. He's laid up with a gunshot wound and, this afternoon, we'll be burying the other three."

For the first time since his descent on the Preston ranch, Mat McCord was speechless; it made for a pleasant change, and Denham was quick to take the initiative.

"Nothin' more you can do here, Mat," he said firmly. "We'd best get back to the ranch."

"We're goin'," growled McCord, moving to his horse. "But not back to Diamond 7. Not rightaway." He swung into his saddle and looked at the widow again, his eyes gleaming maliciously. "From here, we're headed for Bible, and then to Rockin' B. I got some talkin' to do!"

Larry dropped from the rail, but not until the Diamond 7 men were gone from the ranch headquarters. Moving to the sorrel, he announced,

"I'll get back to huntin' strays." His expression was mild, reflecting only polite enquiry, as he matched stares with Holbrook. "'Less there's something you want to ask me."

"Just one question," nodded Holbrook. "Did you and Emerson have to beat up those Diamond 7 hands?"

"Seemed like a good idea at the time," shrugged Larry.

"Sheriff, they were under attack," protested Kate. "They only defended themselves."

"But for a couple of missing horseshoe nails, I might've gotten here in time to prevent that," Holbrook complained. "All right, Valentine, your luck's holding. Seems every time you drifters resort to violence, there are witnesses to support your claim of self-defense."

"Ain't always that way," Larry glumly

assured him, as he mounted the sorrel. "Most times it's us ends up in jail. And the hell of it is we'd be glad to quit fightin'. We'd as soon live peaceable." While wheeling his horse, he frowned perplexedly. "Funny. Nobody ever *believes* that."

For several moments, Holbrook was oblivious to the woman surveying him so intently from the porch. He stood in the yard, hat nudged to the back of his head, wistful eyes following Larry's progress across Wolf Creek range. From the moving horseman, his gaze drifted to that expanse of grazeland and the brush and timber bordering it.

"Ample chores for two good hands, though the herd isn't big," he said, so softly that Kate had to strain her ears. "Not much they can do about the timber, but they could try burning the brush off." A brief pause, then. "Some new calves out there. If they aren't already branded, Valentine had better get busy."

"You understand such things — and you a city man?" she challenged.

"City man?" He turned toward the porch. "Milwaukee-born, ma'am, but raised in the Dakotas. I grew up on ranches, working cattle from the time I was barely twelve years old."

"I guess there's more you want to talk about," she murmured. "Questions . . . ?"

"In my official capacity," he nodded. "You see, until Valentine told me, I just didn't know about the trouble you've been having — trouble from the Council Valley riders?"

"We might as well be comfortable while Mister Emerson's tending your horse," she suggested. "Come join me in the kitchen and I'll fix some coffee."

He stepped up to the porch and about to follow her into the house, paused to sadly study the open doorway.

"It's been so long," he sighed, "I'd almost forgotten how it sounds."

"Pardon?" she frowned, as he entered the kitchen.

"Come on, Sheriff Holbrook," he

said. "Glad to see you. Rest yourself a while. Have some coffee."

"That's pretty much what I said," she nodded, gesturing him to a chair.

"You, Mrs Preston," he said. "But few others. Hardly any in fact." He sank into a chair with his hat in his lap. "Well, that's another matter and no concern of yours. Better we discuss your situation."

"I'll manage better now," she said cheerfully. "Can't say how long they'll stay on, Mister Valentine and his friend. But, for as long as they're here, things'll be better." At the stove, she slid the pot off the flames, deftly reached for cups and saucers and began pouring. "You're a bachelor?"

"I suppose it shows," he said.

"Well, you don't have to stay that way," she said encouragingly, setting the cups on the table seating herself opposite him. "Any time you've had enough of being a lawman, any time you want to get back to ranching, you could settle right here."

As he raised his cup, Holbrook gloomily remarked,

"It's many a long year since I signed on as a hired hand."

"I don't mean as a hired hand," she said impatiently. "I have to marry again and you aren't getting any younger, so why don't we have a preacher or a J.P. say the words over us and just settle in here as husband and wife and — Sheriff Holbrook, you're slopping your coffee . . . !"

5

The Unsuspected

BRECK HOLBROOK was rarely clumsy. Spilling coffee on his vest was embarrassing and uncomfortable, but he could have fared worse; at least he hadn't been perched on the porch-rail. While wiping a lapel with his handkerchief, he eyed the widow incredulously. Did she mean what she was saying? A woman of fairly pleasant appearance, he observed. Reasonably intelligent he had thought — until this moment. Great day in the morning!

"You can't be serious," he chided her.

"I don't fool myself I'm the most eligible woman in Bridger County," she shrugged. "With two kids to raise and trying to run this place all by myself?

No, I don't fool myself. But look at it this way . . . "

"I must be *dreaming* this," he protested. "You're actually trying to *persuade* me?"

"What do you want from marriage anyway?" she challenged. "There's more to it than love and kisses, believe me. Think of all the other reasons. Company, good home cooking, a roof over your head, never being lonely. You'd always know you were wanted and needed. Doesn't that count for anything? And don't be put off by the little you've seen of Jarvis. He's a good boy and Irma's a fine girl."

He seized on her mention of Irma as a means of changing the subject; by now, this was what he needed to do — desperately.

"About your children's education Mrs Preston?"

"The boy's too young for school — maybe they'll take him next year," said Kate. "Irma's good at her studies. Well-behaved too. And . . . "

"I believe I passed your daughter on my way here," he said. "Two girls and a boy, on a mare?"

"She goes to school and back with them all the time," she nodded. "They're the Kipp kids. And I'm beholden to the Kipps . . ."

"Meaning Luke and Chloe Kipp of the Bible Ranch?"

"Yes. If young Jimmy and Rachel weren't coming by to pick up Irma, I'd have to hitch up the team every morning and drive her to the county schoolhouse. She's too young to go in by herself. I'd have to take Jarvis along and — there'd be nobody left here."

"You fear the Kipps will be influenced by Mat McCord?"

"They've been good neighbors up till now. I can't say the same for their hired hands, but Luke and Chloe are kind enough. Still . . ." Kate shrugged helplessly, "if Mister McCord has his way . . ."

"Does he have that much influence

with the other cattlemen hereabouts?" frowned Holbrook.

"You've seen how he is when he's fired up," she reminded him.

"Education is every child's birthright," he declared. "If the Kipps submit to McCord's bullying and withdraw their help, you'd best let me know. Something else will have to be arranged."

"Only natural you'd put a high value on education," she remarked, watching him finish his coffee. "I think myself lucky my folks didn't let me leave school early. It was the same with you, wasn't it?"

He shook his head to her offer of a refill, complimented her on the quality of her coffee and tried to relax. His nerves were steadier now. He had convinced himself there was no danger she would revert to the subject of marriage.

"I was a ranch-worker quite a few years before I decided to improve myself," he confided. "Fortunately I became an enthusiastic reader. Yes, quite a bookworm. That helps, you know. And I took lessons by correspondence."

"That's how you ended up working in a bank," she smiled. "I heard about that. You were a cashier in some town up north until you came to this territory to be sheriff. Well, to get into the banking business, you'd certainly need education."

"All this harrassment, Council Valley riders pestering you," he prodded. "Why wasn't I told? Why didn't you ask my help?"

"You're only one man — with just one deputy," said Kate. "What could you do?"

"Whatever needs doing," he sternly assured her.

"I can send those bunkhouse Romeos running any time I need to," she frowned. "It was — what happened yesterday — those four hard cases trying to . . . "

"Please." He raised a hand. "Don't distress yourself. I'm a man of the world, Mrs Preston, so I do understand."

"I'm a woman of the world with two kids who weren't brought here by any stork," she retorted. "So *I* understand, Sheriff Holbrook. I'm not distressed any more. Just good and mad. They meant to rape me. And, if those Texans hadn't found Jarvis and brought him home . . ."

"Valentine and his partner will be reliable protectors, I'm sure," he said.

"For as long as they stay on," she countered. "But just how long will that be? They're drifters."

"I do realize how difficult it has been for you since the death of your husband," he said carefully.

"No, you don't," she accused. "How could you understand the loneliness, the feeling of being unprotected and at the mercy of any trail-trash coming by? You're just like those Texans. A widow needs a man, a new father for her kids, so has to think of marrying again — and says as much — and you men act as if she's out of her mind.

Mister Emerson was so startled he fell off the porch-rail into my flower-bed. Mister Valentine got angry and made quite a speech. All kinds of warnings — fatherly warnings if you please — as if he's all that old."

"I'd better leave," he said, rising, "before I'm tempted to make the same warning speech you heard from Valentine."

"Well, if you ever change your mind," she shrugged.

"Now, Mrs Preston . . . " he began.

"Or if you get weary of supper in some Cormack cafe and crave home-cooking, come visit us any time you want," she invited. "No obligation — if you're marriage-shy. I'd appreciate cooking for a man again."

"Very kind of you," he muttered, edging to the doorway. "I'll — uh — give it some thought."

When she followed him out to the porch, his horse was tied to the rail, Jarvis and the taller of his heroes standing by.

"Couple nails is all it took," drawled Stretch.

"Thank you," said Holbrook.

"You're welcome," said Stretch. Then, as the lawman descended from the porch and untied the animal, he suggested, "You ought to thank my sidekick too."

"Valentine?" frowned Holbrook.

"No. Him." Stretch nodded to Jarvis. "My other sidekick. He helped."

"I found the hammer and held the nails," the boy gruffly announced.

Holbrook had much to learn about children, but could rise to an occasion. He worked up a genial grin and patted the boy's head.

"I'm obliged to you, boy."

"Welcome," nodded Jarvis.

Eager to be gone, Holbrook swung astride and doffed his hat to the widow.

"I appreciate your hospitality, ma'am. Remember now. Should you be subjected to further indignities, I'll expect you to file formal charges against the parties concerned."

"I guess you'll keep right on being formal," Kate said sadly.

Watching the sheriff ride from the yard, Jarvis mumbled a plea.

"Can I go hunt strays with Uncle Stretch now, Ma? Can I?"

"You're too little for hunting strays — or rattlesnakes," said Kate, "but just the right size for pulling crab grass in the tomato patch. Off with you now."

"Aw, shoot," grouched the boy, as he slouched away. "How come it takes so long to get full growed?"

"I know Mister Valentine wasn't hurt tangling with those cowhands," she said, as Stretch mounted his pinto. "How about you? You were pulled right off your horse. Do you have any bruises, any cuts need tending?"

"No, ma'am." About to return to the herd, he asked, "You gonna keep on callin' us 'Mister'? Most everybody calls us Larry and Stretch."

"All right, Stretch," she smiled. "You and Larry come on back at high noon. That's when we eat lunch here."

"We sure won't forget *that*," he promised, as he nudged his mount to movement.

★ ★ ★

Garth Norman entered Cormack at about the same time the lawman bound for Wolf Creek discovered his mount was throwing a shoe.

Slowly he traveled Main Street, his bearded visage impassive. Through narrowed eyes, ignoring the passers-by, he studied the buildings lining Cormack's busiest thoroughfare. The first to demand his attention was the imposing, triple-storied Penn House, generally regarded as the town's finest hotel. Impressive it undoubtedly was, though any brick or sandstone structure would have appeared more substantial.

"But I'm not complaining, Penn," he reflected. "Clapboard and frame, huh? Wonderful. I wouldn't have it any other way."

Later, passing the Meldrum Reliance

Bank, it pleased him to note he had now traveled four blocks. The hotel and this particular bank were well separated, much to his grim satisfaction.

For his temporary resting place, he chose the small hotel located directly opposite the sheriff's office and county jail, the Brewer House. He checked in there after stabling his horse at a nearby livery and, to the proprietor, described himself as head of the Norman Foundation, small organization formed with the sole object of the reclamation of derelicts and law-breakers.

"I counsel all sinners," he solemnly intoned. "I seek to rescue them from evil and depredation and steer them to the path of righteousness."

"Sounds like a mighty worthy cause, Mister Norman," shrugged the hotel owner. "Your key, sir. Number Three up the stairs."

"I will first seek the abandoned ones . . . " began Norman.

"In the saloons, sure." The hotelkeeper

managed to conceal his amusement. "likeliest hangout for 'em, huh?"

Norman left his gear in his room and began his canvass of the local saloons. Failing to find his henchmen in any of the saloons in the two blocks north of the Brewer House, he tight-reined his impatience and questioned a barkeep. Had there been any trouble in this fine town over the past few days? Thus he learned of the shooting at Sharney's Bar.

"And nobody knows who they are," drawled the barkeep. "Him that got out of it with a busted shoulder, he ain't talkin', ain't tellin' no names. So them three stiffs at the funeral parlor gonna end up in unmarked graves."

The undertaker bought Norman's pitch.

"I have sought to reform many desperadoes these past few years and may have seen these lost ones before."

"You might be able to identify them?" asked the undertaker.

"I can but try," said Norman.

He studied the faces of the deadmen, shook his head sadly, and declared he had never seen them before.

"Can't put names to them?" frowned the undertaker.

"Our paths never crossed," lied Norman.

The arrival of a peddler's wagon a short time later caused a few eyebrows to rise; such rigs were rarely seen nowadays. Fulbright, cheerfully ignoring the resentful stares of the town's resident merchants, made a slow progress along Main, nodding affably to passers-by, doffing his derby to the womenfolk and missing nothing. He noted the location of the Penn House and the Reliance Bank, sighted a familiar figure on the street porch of the Brewer House and, after stalling the wagon in a side street, strolled to that nondescript establishment opposite the county jail.

The council of war was held in Norman's room, Fulbright maintaining his unruffled demeanor, Norman giving vent to his disgust, both of them keeping their voices low.

"Had I taken more time to find the kind of men I need, I wouldn't have chosen riff-raff like Garrett and his friends," the bearded man said bitterly. "Four trigger-happy morons. I couldn't rely on them to hold still until I got here. They just had to make trouble — and it cost them."

"How about the sore and sorry guest in the calaboose?" asked Fulbright.

"Garrett himself," scowled Norman. "I recognized the dead men at the funeral parlor. His sidekicks."

"But naturally you aren't calling it off," guessed Fulbright.

A nerve quivered at Norman's cheekbone.

"There'll be no peace for me until . . . !"

"Yeah, okay, so be grateful I know where to find the Emhardt boys," said Fulbright, rising.

"Yes," nodded Norman. "You'd best get started."

"Howabout that Reliance Bank, huh?" Fulbright chuckled derisively. "Stone foundations if you please, and its floor a good three feet above ground. Hell, it's gonna be so damn *easy* . . . !"

"Provided we make our play at night," stressed Norman. "Provided that part of town is deserted — all attention fixed on the Penn House. We need that diversion. And that's why we need those extra men."

"You'll have 'em soon enough," promised Fulbright.

"Of course you've not seen the safe at the Reliance," frowned Norman.

"I'll take a look at it rightaway but, like I'm always telling you, Meldrum's safe will be no problem," said Fulbright. "They haven't built one I can't crack."

"Even so . . . " began Norman.

"All right, don't worry about it," said Fulbright. "I'll stop by to change a fifty on my way out of town."

At the bank, while a teller made change for him, the bogus peddler flicked a casual glance to the area behind the cashier's cage, noted the brand-name on the old safe and laughed inwardly. A Winthrop & Steiner. After all these years, so many new and improved models available, the Reliance was still using a Winthrop & Steiner. To Fulbright, it just went to prove frontier bankers weren't exactly the big brains of the world of commerce and finance.

His triumphant mood prevailed after he had quit Cormack and was following the regular trail toward a turn-off. It was then that he encountered a town-bound rider who signaled him to halt. He obeyed that signal, undismayed by the metal star gleaming on Breck Holbrook's vest, his bland grin a fixture.

"'Morning. Fulbright's the name. And you'll be county sheriff, right?"

"Sheriff Holbrook," nodded the lawman, reining up to look the rig over.

"Pegged you for a boss-lawman right

off," drawled Fulbright. "Knew you couldn't be just a deputy. You got that look of authority. Well now, something I can do for you, sir?"

"Something you can do for yourself," said Holbrook, fishing out a cigar. "You passed through Cormack?" Fulbright nodded. "Didn't set yourself up to peddle your wares, I hope?"

"Well, no," said Fulbright. "Just looking the town over, you know? Planned on coming back in a couple days. Got to go pick up some extra stock before I . . . "

"Do yourself a favor," advised Holbrook. "Don't try setting up your store on wheels anywhere in the county seat. That way, you'll stay out of trouble. There's a county ordinance prohibiting itinerant peddlers hawking their wares inside town."

"Me and my luck," shrugged Fulbright.

"Come now, Mister Fulbright, this couldn't be the first time you've come up against such a regulation," said Holbrook. He lit his cigar and grinned mirthlessly. "I'm sure you know the situation in all the well-established towns. We have ample stores, emporiums selling all kinds of merchandise, the storekeepers competing for business. So, obviously, a transient with a wagonload of cheap merchandise poses a threat to local trade."

"You're right, I've run into this kind of thing before," nodded Fulbright. "Too bad. I was hoping . . . "

"The regulation applies only to Cormack itself," offered Holbrook. "You're welcome to try your luck at the local cattle spreads and homesteads or peddle your merchandise along any trails leading to the county seat, just so long as you stay outside the town limits."

"Well now, I sure thank you for steering me right, Sheriff," Fulbright said genially. "Reckon that's just what I'll do." He raised a hand in cheery salute. "Nice talking to you, sir."

He kicked off his brake and drove

on to be forgotten by Holbrook. The sheriff of Bridger County was preoccupied, but no longer brooding on the prejudice of Cormack's upper crust. A couple of irritatingly casual drifters, only recently arrived in his bailiwick, were making their presence felt in no uncertain terms; three hard cases dead, another wounded and in custody, three Diamond 7 waddies somewhat the worse for having tangled with them. He was not, however, worrying about those rock-fisted Texans.

"I oughtn't be worrying at all," he chided himself as he rode on toward Cormack. "Least of all about an eccentric widow who has never heard of tact or discretion. Confound the woman. What's to become of her? The hell with it. Not my problem."

* * *

For several days thereafter, the county seat and the regions beyond knew no violence. The atmosphere was devoid of tension, no citizen suspecting this was the lull before the storm.

At the Wolf Creek spread, the Kipp children called for Irma as usual. Questioned by Irma's mother, young Jimmy Kipp reported on the visit of Mr Mat McCord. He hadn't been allowed to get close enough to listen, but his pa and Mr McCord had sure wrangled. As near as he could understand, Mr McCord was giving orders and pa giving Mr McCord a big argument. Also, he heard Ma say Mr McCord ought to be ashamed.

"That's something in Luke Kipp's favor," Kate remarked to the Texans, after the children had ridden away. "Well, they're good church-going people, the Kipps. Full of charity, but not weak."

"Sounds like ol' Mat bit off more'n he could chaw at Bible," opined Stretch.

"After spring round-up, I'm hoping Luke Kipp will offer to take my best steers to the railhead," said Kate. "There'll only be . . . ?"

"I'd reckon a hundred and twenty head," said Larry. "But prime stock, Kate. They'll bring top dollar, count on that."

"He's just bound to offer," she predicted. "Why, Bible will be driving twenty-five hundred head. Luke Kipp's herders will hardy notice another hundred and twenty."

To Kate's secret disappointment, there was no follow-up visit from the county sheriff, but her daughter gleefully reported he had come to the schoolyard to speak with her.

"Just to talk to you, honey? Well, what did he say?"

"Asked if Jimmy and Rachel were still fetching me to school and back. And, Mama, he said 'By your leave' before he lit his cigar."

"That was very polite of the sheriff. He ask you anything else?"

"Asked me if I enjoy English lessons. I told him English is my favorite lesson

151

and he said that's fine because if you learn to talk properly, everybody knows you're a lady. I like the sheriff, Mama. He's awful handsome."

Twenty-four hours after Cal Fulbright's return to Bridger County, five strangers in ranch-hands' rig rode into Cormack. Checking into the Brewer House, Dex and Burt Emhardt described themselves and their cohorts as horse-breakers bound for a big Colorado ranch in need of their services. And, within a half-hour of their arrival, these five hard cases were receiving their instructions from Garth Norman in a private room of an uptown gambling house.

Friday morning, Norman visited Fulbright at his camp a mile west of the county seat for a final conference. Side by side in the brush beside the campsite they squatted, talking softly.

"It's set up for tomorrow night," Norman announced. "I've talked it over with the Emhardts and they know exactly what they have to do."

"Told you we could count on those jaspers," grinned Fulbright. "For a piece of that bank loot, they'll get the job done, you'll see. Diversion? Hell! Some diversion. Won't be one citizen cares a damn what happens down around the Reliance Bank." He nodded approvingly. "Saturday night, huh?"

"The hotel keeper happened to mention tomorrow is payday for the ranch-hands of this area," said Norman. "That means extra men in town by the time we're ready to do. A bigger crowd. The townfolk and the cattlemen will jam the street in front of the hotel. There'll be volunteers fighting the fire and a lot of confusion, enough of it to keep the law busy and distract attention from the downtown area."

"You could've picked any other building uptown, but no," muttered Fulbright. "It has to be the Penn hotel." He chuckled harshly. "He'll be wiped out. And he'll never know who set him up."

"*I'll* know," scowled Norman.

"Listen, are you ever gonna tell me why you hate his guts?" demanded Fulbright. "You're squaring accounts, you keep saying. Is it all that personal with you two?"

"Emory Penn probably hasn't spared a thought for me these past five years," Norman said through clenched teeth, "He's forgotten me, and that's fine by me. But *I* don't forget."

"You ever gonna tell me . . . ?" Fulbright began again.

"I'll tell you," said Norman. "And then you'll not ask me again. Understood?"

"Whatever you say," nodded Fulbright.

"He was a hotel clerk in Rivette, Nebraska, five years ago — the town where I stood trial . . . "

That was how Norman's story began, his account of a one-man bank robbery that had backfired. Single-handed, he had taken $10,000 from a Rivette

154

bank and, while hunted by a posse, had cached his loot. Apprehended and taken back to Rivette to stand trial, he protested his innocence.

"I was a mighty persuasive talker even then. The lawyer they appointed to defend me, I certainly had him convinced. Mistaken identity was our claim. I was masked when I took that bank, so how could the witnesses positively identify me?"

"Prosecuting attorney was a spell-binder," guessed Fulbright. "Your lawyer just wasn't good enough."

"The prosecutor didn't decide my fate." Norman's eyes were red-rimmed; his voice shook with emotion. "I later learned I had Penn to blame for the guilty verdict and my five years in that territorial prison. Penn was foreman of the jury. Half of those twelve good men and true were inclined to give me the benefit of the doubt, but Penn bullied them till they saw it his way."

"Convicted man never knows what's said in the jury room," argued Fulbright.

"How'd you find out who voted against you?"

"One of those coincidences," said Norman. "A year after I began my hitch in prison, one of those jurors, a blacksmith name of Hartley, killed a man in a saloon fight. He was convicted of manslaughter and ended up in Block Five at the big pen." He grinned coldly. "Recognized me, of course. And we eventually got to talking of my trial. Emory Penn didn't like my looks, my style, any part of me, Hartley told me. Considered himself a reliable judge of character, insisted there was no doubt about my guilt. Masked or not, I was the right size. And the bank staff insisted mine was the voice they heard ordering them to unlock the safe. Oh, yes. Penn carried the day. Not the prosecutor. Not the judge. Just Penn — so righteous — so persuasive."

"From clerk of a Nebraska hotel to owner of his own hotel in Wyoming is quite a step," remarked Fulbright.

156

"He'd already left Rivette with his wife before Hartley's trial," said Norman. "A relative died and left him enough money to establish himself in his own business. It took me a little time, but I can be patient — as you well know."

"So you finally tracked him to Cormack," grinned Fulbright. "And no chance he'll remember you?"

"How can he remember me?" challenged Norman. "It's been five years. I was cleanshaven and short-haired when I had my day in court. Even if we came face to face, it's not likely he'd recognize me."

"Not much chance he'll see you anyway," opined Fulbright. His gaze strayed to the wagon, and not for the first time. The rig was positioned a safe distance from the campfire, but he was sensitive to changes in wind direction. "When will they be out here to pick up the coal-oil?"

"Sometime after sundown tomorrow," said Norman.

"And — uh — just when . . . ?" began Fulbright.

"We'll meet behind the bank, you and I, at quarter of eleven," said Norman.

"Right," grunted Fulbright. "And I'll fetch everything we're gonna need. Couple crowbars. Couple valises. You know . . . " he paused to chuckle elatedly, "there's strong chance nobody'll know the bank's been looted before opening time Monday!"

"We'll still be around anyway, neither of us showing signs of quitting this territory," Norman reminded him. "The Emhardts and their friends will head south during all the excitement, but we'll not budge."

"They start lighting matches same time we meet behind the bank," guessed Fulbright.

"Same time," nodded Norman. "I calculate we'll be into the bank by eleven . . . "

"Three minutes is all the time I'll need for picking the lock of that Winthrop and Steiner," Fulbright interjected. "Push-over. I don't even need a special tool. Just wire."

"In by eleven, out by eleven-fifteen," opined Norman. "Or it may only need ten minutes."

"Some helluva deal," enthused Fulbright.

"By Sunday morning, Penn will be out of business," muttered Norman. "He'll console himself that his savings are safe — until Monday morning."

"Dumb bastard'll probably shoot himself," shrugged Fulbright.

Midday Saturday, at lunch with her husband in their private suite on the hotel's top floor, the slender and sedate Albertina Penn issued a reminder.

"The Archands are dining with us tonight."

"Dinner and whist," grinned the hotelowner. "Well, it would have to be Cleave and Jessie, wouldn't it, my dear?"

"The only other whist-players in the territory," she nodded. "Our favorite pastime, and we can never persuade our other friends to take it up. I've talked to the Robinsons, the Kellaways, the Suttons . . . "

"Another pleasant evening with good friends," predicted Penn.

"Unless Cleave spoils everything — as he did the last time we got together," frowned Albertina.

Emory Penn fixed a cautious eye on his still attractive wife. He was showing the bulk, the thickening waistline accepted as a side effect of affluence, balding too, but a well-groomed man and, like his friend the mayor, gregarious at heart. If it were up to Emory Penn and Mayor Cleave Archand, Cormack society would have been less class-conscious. Their wives, however, had the last word on that subject.

"I thought our last whist party was pleasant enough," he remarked.

"Until Cleave insisted on mentioning Sheriff Holbrook," sniffed his spouse. "From then on, Jessie was furious with him, and I certainly don't blame her.

Cleave's timing is terrible. Imagine mentioning that person in the middle of the game!"

"That person is our duly appointed senior law officer," he gently argued.

"But a common gunfighter," she insisted. "That is the most distasteful aspect of frontier society. Haven't I said it before?"

"Many times," sighed Penn.

"Few — if any — presentable persons become sheriffs of cattle communities," she complained. "They are invariably no better than the rogues they are paid to control. They are, for the most part, distinguishable from the riff-raff only by the badges they wear."

"That's not an accurate assessment of Breck Holbrook," he protested. "Tina, my dear, you don't know the man."

"Do you?" she challenged. "Admit it. You've only met him the once."

"Well, sure," he nodded. "But I found him to be well-spoken and courteous and — Cleave speaks highly of him. We should remember that, less than two years ago, Holbrook was in the banking business."

"His reputation," retorted Albertina, "was not built on his efficiency as a banking man. Cleave chose him for his skill with a pistol."

"All right, all right," shrugged Penn. "Let's not get into an argument. And I doubt Cleave would make the same mistake twice. He won't mention the sheriff tonight."

At Wolf Creek, the Texans kept busy that day. As well as tending the prime Preston stock, they took care of a few repairs around the ranch buildings with willing if inept assistance from Kate's children. Always patient with the small fry, they were in relaxed mood when, around 5 p.m., Kate climbed to the toprail of the corral wherein they were currying their horses.

She addressed them firmly.

"No arguments about this."

"About what, ma'am?" enquired Stretch.

"After supper it would please me to

see you saddle your animals and ride," she declared.

"How d'you like that?" Larry said poker-faced. "She's weary of us already, so now she's firin' us."

"Enough of your jokes, Larry," she chided. "How can I fire you when you won't let me pay for all the work you're doing?"

"Told you before," he shrugged. "We're happy to hang around a while and work for our keep. We got all the dinero we need."

"Good bunks and the kind of chow you dish up is pay enough," Stretch assured her.

"That's charity, and I did agree to it," she nodded. "But you haven't been to town in quite a few days."

"So?" challenged Larry. "What's Cormack got that we need?"

"Cormack has what every working ranch-hand craves on paydays," she pointed out. "Saloons, gambling houses, a dance hall, a theatre — places you can go to unwind, to have a little fun.

You don't have to be stuck here all the time. And I can manage without you till tomorrow morning. We don't feel so nervous now, the kids and I. Word has gotten around and those Council Valley hands are staying far clear of Wolf Creek."

"Well . . . " began Stretch.

"You owe it to yourselves," she pleaded. "Do it. Take the night off, and then I won't feel so guilty."

"What d'you say, Mister Valentine suh?" asked Stretch. "You crave a little pleasurin', a little socializin'?"

"Well now, Mister Emerson suh, we oughtn't argue with a lady, ought we?" drawled Larry. "Can't have her feelin' guilty on our account."

"I'll feel a whole lot happier, knowing you're enjoying yourselves," smiled Kate.

That was why Larry and Stretch started for the county seat right after supper. To enjoy themselves.

6

Act of Treachery

AT 8 p.m., when the Texans sauntered into Sharney's Bar, barkeep Jerry Ness was waiting on a half-dozen cowhands, two from Diamond 7, one Rocking B man and three Bible riders. Breasting the bar, they traded friendly nods with the proprietor. The local ranch-hands sized them up, but not challengingly, and Stretch was moved to remark to the barkeep.

"Safe enough for us to drink here — 'less lightnin' *do* strike in the same place twice."

Ness grinned and set two glasses on the bar. Sharney, interrupting his conversation with a couple of cronies, saluted the tall men and assured them,

"That was the worst trouble we have

had here, and it just couldn't happen again."

While paying for their drinks, Larry ran an eye over the patrons and spotted a familiar face; the sheriff of Bridger County was seated alone at a rear corner table.

"You feel like socializin' with the law?" he asked his partner.

"What can we lose?" shrugged Stretch. "Only two things he can say. 'Come join me' or 'leave me alone'."

They carried their glasses to Holbrook's table. Rousing from his reverie, he raised his eyes, nodded absently and gestured for them to seat themselves. While doing so, Larry declared.

"A man ought never drink alone if he's of troubled mind."

"Bad for his disposition," nodded Stretch. "He could end up lonesome drunk — which ain't no fun at all."

"Specially if he wears a badge," Larry pointed out.

"Better to be friendly drunk," offered Stretch.

"Let me set you straight on two points," said Holbrook. "I am not of troubled mind right now. Just thoughtful. And I *never* get drunk." He stubbed out the last two inches of a cigar and surveyed them with renewed interest. "By accident, just a few hours ago, I learned something of you hot-shots. Happened to be checking the files compiled by the late Sheriff Martinson, trying to identify my prisoner. And what do you suppose I found?"

"A file about us," guessed Larry. "Warnin's from the army and the U.S. marshal's office . . . "

"And a dozen other county lawmen," said Holbrook.

"And a whole mess of hogwash cut out of newspapers," sighed Stretch.

"But you didn't find any 'Wanted' dodgers on us," said Larry. "Trouble-shooters they call us."

"We don't much enjoy that," muttered Stretch.

"You needn't be on the defensive,"

shrugged Holbrook. "I haven't been a lawman all that long, you know. Certainly not long enough to work up any animosity toward independents like you. If a private citizen apprehends an outlaw, that's fine by me." Sipping his whiskey, he casually enquired, "How are things at Wolf Creek?"

"The lady ain't so nervous now," said Larry.

"I just meant the ranch — generally," frowned Holbrook. "I wasn't asking about the lady in particular."

"We're caught up on chores," drawled Stretch. "It's so peaceful out there, she said go to town and have a little fun."

"The kids're real fine," offered Larry.

"Quite a change for a couple of fiddle-foots," suggested Holbrook. "According to your record, you rarely stay in one place for an indefinite period."

"We'll hang around Wolf Creek maybe a few more weeks," said Stretch. "Quite a lady, Mrs Preston.

But we ain't leery of her no more."

"Not since I finally convinced her it's no use proposin' at us," grinned Larry.

"That's not funny," complained Holbrook. "She made me the same offer. And it's not funny." He took another pull at his whiskey. "Helluva thing — a woman being so desperate."

"Well now, I don't reckon she'll stay a widow the rest of her life," said Larry. "I'll allow she's pushy and tries too hard . . . "

"Far too hard," winced Holbrook. "No preamble. No warning. I was talking with her only a minute or two before she raised the subject of marriage."

"She'll finally win herself another man," Larry predicted.

"I don't see how she can fail," said Holbrook, wincing, again. "But, damn it, no woman should take such risks. Too dangerous. She could end up with an opportunist, some lazy good-for-nothing who'll take advantage of her."

"That'd be a real shame," remarked Stretch.

"Won't happen," Larry said encouragingly. "Not if some interested hombre keeps a friendly eye on her."

Some 45 minutes later, when the Texans ambled along to a larger saloon, the Penns and the Archands had finished supper and were settling down to their favorite pastime in the handsomely-furnished parlor on the hotel's top floor, and the Emhardt brothers and their cohorts were on their way back from Cal Fulbright's camp. The peddler's wagon had been emptied of its incendiary cargo, a half-dozen cans of coal-oil, and now those cans were slung to the saddles of five rogues every inch as treacherous as Norman himself.

At 10 o'clock, Holbrook was walking patrol and finding Main Street to be no noisier than should be expected on a Saturday night. Council Valley hands were here in force, but the payday revelry wasn't out of hand; he anticipated a trouble-free night.

As was his habit on such occasions, Aaron Dubb was watching the street from his favorite chair on the law office porch ready to bestir himself should violence erupt. He didn't notice the dapper man in the checkered suit, but then the unobtrusive arrival was one of Cal Fulbright's many talents.

At 10.30, Norman and Fulbright were in position under the Meldrum Reliance Bank, preparing to crowbar floorboards and force entry. Behind the Penn House and in the alleys to either side, their five aides were taking their time dousing the outer walls, emptying cans of their inflammable contents. It was dark in those side alleys, but they took no chances on being sighted by locals passing by along the main stem.

The hulking Emhardt brothers ventured to the street-end of the southside alley and peered toward the hotel entrance.

"One can left — and maybe that

lobby's empty," muttered the elder brother.

"There'll be a night-clerk," opined Burt Emhardt.

"Even so," shrugged Dex Emhardt. "It'd sure pleasure me to start this place burnin' inside as well as outside," He grinned callously. "The inside stairs, know what I mean?"

"They'll be leapin' outa windows," chuckled Burt.

"Close enough to eleven o'clock," said Dex. "C'mon, let's do it."

After ensuring their movements would be unobserved, they stepped up to the porch and entered the lobby. The only person in sight, the night-clerk, was catnapping and an easy mark. Burt Emhardt hurried to the reception desk to bring his Colt's barrel down on the man's head with crushing force while his brother uncapped the can and emptied coal-oil over the bottom steps of the staircase. Roughly, Burt hauled his victim to the corner left of the entrance and dumped him there.

The can was tossed aside after a stream of oil had been spilled from the stairs to the entrance. The brothers then stepped out to the porch, scanned the immediate area and traded mirthless grins. Dex Emhardt scratched a match, flicked it over a shoulder and, with his brother at his heels, scuttled into the side alley.

In the wider alley running level with Main on the west side, they rejoined their cohorts. The outer walls behind and both sides of the hotel were afire now.

"That's it," grunted Burt. "Time to go?"

"You know it," nodded Dex. "Move your butts, boys. We're on our way."

After following Norman through the jagged opening in the bank floor, Fulbright discarded his crowbar, tossed the empty valises toward the safe and fished out a stub of candle.

"Shades are down," he pointed out. "Safe enough to use this."

"I make it eleven sharp," said

173

Norman. "Any minute now, we'll hear the outcry from uptown — if the Emhardts and their friends have done their job."

"I told you," grinned Fulbright. "You can count on 'em."

Hunkered by the safe, he lit his candle and went to work.

Breck Holbrook was about to leave the bar, nodding so-long to Sharney and the barkeep, when the alarm was raised. He heard somebody shout 'Fire!' and, as he started for the batwings, the louder sound smote his ears, the clanging of a bell; Cormack's volunteer fire-fighters were turning out in force. He cursed bitterly and hurried outside just in time to see the Texans crossing Main Street at a hard run. Then his shocked gaze switched to the Penn House and he was following them as fast as his legs could carry him.

The trouble-shooters were reacting automatically. It wasn't bravado that compelled them to unstrap and discard their side arms and flop into horse-troughs, completely immersing themselves. They were doing what came naturally. Holbrook's jaw sagged as the saturated figures struggled from the troughs and made straight for the blazing entrance of the hotel. He yelled after them while signaling the fire-rig.

Oblivious to the lawman's warning, the Texans charged into the lobby. It was Stretch who, only by chance, glimpsed the night-clerk's left foot. While Larry warily appraised the blazing stairs, he hurried to the corner to lift the body.

"Wasn't fire nor smoke killed this jasper!" he called. "His skull's stove in!"

"Get him out of here," urged Larry. "And tell Holbrook we're checkin' upstairs."

The main entrance was a wall of flame. To move the body out and alert Holbrook, the taller Texan demolished a front window with a chair. He passed the body through to a couple of sweating fire-fighters, one of whom gasped a plea.

"Better get out of there, big feller!"

"Might be folks trapped upstairs," Stretch retorted. "My partner and me gonna . . . "

"Don't nobody else come inside!" bellowed Larry. "There'll be people droppin' out of windows, so you'd better be ready! Get tarps, blankets — anything!"

With Stretch tagging, he leapt over the first three steps and barged up to the landing. There, panting heavily, they paused to glance backward. That first section of the staircase was now well and truly afire.

"Did we — move through *all that*!" Stretch asked incredulously.

"Not all of it," muttered Larry.

"You sure?" challenged Stretch.

"Still alive, ain't we?" shrugged Larry. "C'mon, let's keep climbin'. I figure the folks on the ground floor'll make it. They only have to climb out of the windows. It's them up higher gonna need help."

They found the second floor corridor filling with guests emerging from the rooms to either side, most of them in panic, most of them in their nightclothes.

"The outside stairs are afire!" a woman cried.

"Follow me, everybody!" a male guest summoned his courage and started toward the Texans. "We'll have to get out through the lobby!"

"Can't be done, friend," warned Larry. "Staircase is gonna break up any moment and the whole lobby's burnin'."

"Well — hell!" protested another man. "We can't just stay here and . . . !"

"Hang onto your nerves, folks," urged Stretch, and he actually worked up a reassuring grin. "There'll be another way out — right, runt?"

"Thanks," growled Larry. "I needed that."

"Think nothin' of it," shrugged Stretch.

Smoke was invading that corridor and the guests in fear for their lives when Larry darted into a bedroom and across to an open window to check the northside alley. The firestairs were ablaze, but some hardy citizen, undeterred by dancing flames and flying sparks, had driven a wagonload of hay into the alley and was yelling,

"Everybody jump!"

"Some of you'll make it this way," Larry called over his shoulder. "C'mon! Ladies first!"

Four women were helped through the window by the Texans and unceremoniously dropped to the hay, an undignified descent but a soft landing. One man followed the women, and then this means of escape had to be abandoned; predictably, the hay caught fire. There was nought the plucky driver could do but hustle the team into the centre of Main Street, unhitch them and abandon the vehicle. The man struggled from the hay with his nightshirt afire, but had the good sense to remove the garment. Unscathed and naked as the day he was born, he ran for the nearest cover.

Lacking the courage to leap from top floor windows, a dozen or more guests had descended to the second floor to swell the ranks of those relying on the tall strangers to devise a means of escape. Larry investigated a room on the south side and, staring down to the alley, yelled to the half-dozen men unrolling a tarp,

"Front wall's burnin'!" one of them called up to him. "Back and both sides too. The boys're doin' their damndest, but you can forget the firestairs!"

"We got near twenty people up here — maybe more!" yelled Larry. "Get that tarp stretched and stand by!"

"Hustle 'em, mister!" came the terse rejoinder. "They move fast — or they fry!"

"Let's go, ladies," Stretch called, and terrified women began filing past him to the window.

"Feet-first," Larry said encouragingly, seizing the first flustered female. "Nothin' to it, ma'am. You don't have to look down. Just close your eyes and drop."

The tarp was stretched directly below the window, gripped tight by the volunteers, when the first woman dropped. One by one, the Texans eased the others out of the window and, screaming, they plummeted to the canvas. The rescuers could spare no time for niceties. After hitting the canvas, each woman was tipped off unceremoniously and the canvas stretched to catch the next faller.

Then came the men heavier, but less inclined to protest. As the last one dropped the volunteers urged the Texans to get out while there was still time.

"We could quit now," Stretch remarked to Larry. "If only . . . "

"Uh huh," grunted Larry. "If only we knew for sure."

"That's the hell of it," complained

Stretch. "Might be more people upstairs."

Flames were licking about the window when Larry thrust his head out to call to the volunteers.

"We'll be checkin' the top floor!"

They pulled their sodden bandanas up to mask their noses and mouths as they re-entered the second floor corridor. Visibility was nil, so thick was the smoke. On the other side, flames belched from every doorway. They trudged to their left an, bedeviled by the heat, kept moving until they reached another staircase. Always the optimist, Stretch commented.

"Our luck's still holdin'."

"I know what you mean," said Larry, grinning behind his bandana. "At least we found the *up* staircase. Other one'll be burnin' fierce by now."

They climbed to the top floor corridor to find every door open except one. As Larry moved toward that closed door, Stretch checked the other rooms.

"All empty," he reported, catching up with his partner. "And — listen — I peeked out a couple windows — both sides."

"How's the scenery?" asked Larry, trying the door.

"Ain't purty," shrugged Stretch. "Walls're afire."

Larry turned the knob, shoved the door open and moved into a tastefully-appointed room into which smoke was only now filtering. Playing cards were scattered on the carpet. A small table had been placed atop a larger table, a chair atop the small table, making it possible for the occupants to reach the manhole and climb through to the roof. They stared up to the opening.

"Am I reading your mind, runt?" frowned Stretch. "They knew they couldn't make it downstairs . . . "

"And they weren't about to jump," nodded Larry. "Not from this high up."

"So the only place they could head for was the roof," said Stretch.

"Do I have to say it?" asked Larry, shrugging resignedly. "The roof is the only place *we* can head now. You first, ol' buddy."

For Holbrook and old Aaron it had been quite a struggle, but the Saturday night crowd of gawking ranch-hands and excited townfolk was finally under control and co-operating, lining the sidewalk opposite the doomed hotel, no longer impeding the fire-fighters. While Aaron mingled with the bucket-brigade and the gang working the pump for the hose, his boss hunkered beside the medico administering to burn victims, the lean, quietly-spoken Maurice Edwards.

"I know what's on your mind," Edwards assured him. "Same question's on my mind, but we should stop trying to guess. We aren't architects or engineers."

"So far the top storey is surviving, but it can't last," fretted Holbrook. "Our volunteers can't do any more than they're doing. The ground floor and the floor above are near gutted — so how long can that top storey hold up? And Aaron claims he glimpsed people on the roof."

To their credit, the four people on the roof were striving to retain their nerve, the women as much as the men.

"I'm sure they know we're up here," Penn said as calmly as he was able. "It's only a matter of time. They'll devise some means of getting us off this roof and . . . "He fished out a handkerchief to mop at his brow. "Cleave — Jessie — I'm desperately sorry for . . . "

"Enough of that, Emory," chided the mayor.

"As if anybody could hold you responsible," frowned Jessie, linking arms with the apprehensive Albertina. "We accepted your invitation as we've done so often before. You can hardly blame yourself."

"Accidents happen," shrugged Archand.

"Can't *somebody* do *something*?" begged Albertina.

"It's only a matter of time," said her husband.

"You said that before," she complained.

For a few more moments, four representatives of upper class Cormack stood by the manhole, the mayor and his host a distinguished-looking duo in their custom-tailored evening clothes, their wives resplendent in their silken gowns; the Penns and the Archands always dressed for dinner and whist. They then loosed startled gasps. A head and shoulders had risen from below. In a pronounced southern drawl a greeting was voiced.

"Howdy there folks. If you got no objection my partner and me gonna get you out of this fix." Stretch added somewhat lamely, as he pulled himself free of the manhole and rose to his full height, "Well — somehow."

Larry clambered through, got to his feet and, after according the gaping quartet a casual nod, hurried across to the roofs front side to stare down into the street.

"What on earth . . . ?" began Jessie.

"How did you get here?" demanded Penn.

"Same way as you," shrugged Stretch. "Up through the manhole."

"That's not what I mean," frowned Penn.

"Well, we come in through the lobby and made it up the first flight of stairs," Stretch explained. "But then the stairs and the whole lobby got to be like thirty square feet of hell — beggin' your pardon ladies — so we just kept comin'. We been shovin' folks out of windows and stuff like that. Just tryin' to be useful, you know?" He called to Larry. "How's it look runt?"

"They can see me and that's somethin'," Larry replied. "Listen, while I'm hollerin' to 'em, you check the north and south sides." Leaning over the parapet, he bellowed to the men far below. "Get a ladder up to us! Longest you can find!"

Old Aaron promptly whirled and

186

growled instructions to some of his cronies.

"Leroy and Sid, you fetch a long ladder. Cliff and Abe, we're gonna need rope. Two kinds, hear? A line — like a lariat for instance — and some thicker rope, stronger."

"How're we gonna get it up to 'em?"

"Can be done, boys. And I know how."

With that, the deputy headed for the law office with speed belying his years. He was back by the time the ladder and ropes had been procured, armed with bow and arrows. At his orders, the lariat was knotted to the thicker rope. He secured its other end to an arrow and, realizing his intention, Larry yelled encouragement.

"That'll do it, Aaron! Give it your best shot!"

People held their breath as the old Indian scout back-stepped a few paces, braced himself, fitted the arrow to his bow, aimed for the roof and drew back the bowstring. Seconds after releasing the projectile, he scampered clear of the rope. And this was a night for miracles. Despite the weight of the line attached to it, the arrow didn't start its downward arc until it cleared the parapet. Penn and Archand pulled their wives clear. Stretch sidestepped nimbly and, as the arrow fell to the roof and began moving backward, encumbered by the line, checked it by the simple process of falling on it.

"Okay, I got it," Larry called to him. "Get rid of the arrow and I'll have 'em tie their end to the ladder."

"If the line's long enough," countered Stretch.

"It's long enough," growled Larry.

Down the blackened, smoking facade of the building they lowered the rope. When it could be lowered no further and was dangling well above ground level, Holbrook cursed impatiently and ran to the nearest vehicle, a buckboard. Scrambling to the seat he whipped up the team and drove the rig onto the sidewalk, stalling it directly under the rope's end.

"Now the ladder — quickly!" he ordered, rising to stand on the seat.

He was sweating and harassed by the time he had knotted the rope to a top rung. As he drove the buckboard clear, men signaled the Texans to start hauling. Penn and Archand promptly lent their aid to that chore and, in a matter of moments, the rope was snaking over the roof and the Texans grasping the ladder's top end, hauling it up and over. They detached the rope and, bluntly, Stretch declared,

"They'll have to try it that side." He gestured to his left. "Next roof over there is a mite lower'n this'n, but the ladder might reach it. Other side — no chance."

"All right," nodded Larry. As they toted the ladder past the civic leaders and their womenfolk, he called a question. " Who's your neighbor on your northside?"

"Krantz's bakery," offered Penn. "A

double-storied place. Do you really think . . . ?"

"Ask me in a minute," said Larry.

From the north edge of the roof, the Texans eased the ladder out and downward to the roof of the next building. The slant presented no problems, Larry decided. With the base of the ladder firm on the lower roof and this end steadied by Texas muscle, the Penns and their guests could make it. But not if they paused to debate their chances; flames were surging up the hotel's north wall.

"It'll be okay, ma'am," Stretch said encouragingly, crooking a finger at the mayor's wife, "You first."

"Hurry, Jessie," urged Archand. "No arguments."

"I'll go first if everybody insists," said Jessie. "But this is no time for modesty. In this gown, I'd be at a serious disadvantage."

To Albertina's horror, she unfastened and peeled off her gown. Her husband snatched it from her and hurled it

190

to the bakery roof and then, with help from the Texans, she moved out onto the ladder and gingerly began the descent.

"I could never do *that*!" gasped Albertina.

But now the room below was afire and portion of the roof igniting. The hotelowner's wife abruptly reversed her decision when flame darted up and caught the hem of her gown. Archand called a warning and, with no help from her haggard husband, she was out of the garment within seconds of the material's flaring.

"Other lady's made it to the bakery," reported Larry. "You next, ma'am. Hustle now!"

"It'll be all right, Tina," muttered Penn. "Don't be afraid."

"I'm not afraid!" she wailed, as Stretch helped her lower her feet to the fourth rung. "I'm *terrified*! And — the only reason I'm — doing this . . . !"

"Nothing else you can do," nodded Archand. "Go carefully now, Tina.

You'll be safe in a few moments."

Despite her state of fear, aggravated by the rising flames already licking at the ladder, Albertina Penn managed to travel rung by rung to the safety of the bakery roof and Jessie's comforting embrace.

"Ladder'll catch fire in a couple more minutes, gents," warned Larry. "You'll have to move faster'n the ladies."

"Emory, let's have none of that nonsense about the captain being last to leave the sinking ship," growled Archand. "I know you're a year and a half my senior. On your way, old friend."

Penn had the good sense not to look downward when he swung off the roof-edge and got his feet to the ladder. He climbed down to the roof of the other building with his teeth clenched and his nerves in turmoil. The hotel's north side was a wall of flame now, the onlookers fearing the whole structure would collapse at any moment. Reaching the roof, he flopped to his knees, gripped the ladder hard and called to the mayor.

"*Hurry*, Cleave!"

Archand was tight-lipped until beginning his descent. Then, aghast, he stared at the two men watching from above.

"This ladder's burning already!" he cried. "Even if I make it — what happens to *you*?"

"Mister, you pick a helluva time to stop and ask questions," chided Stretch.

"Move your ass!" roared Larry.

Archand descended two more rungs of the ladder. The next rung his left hand touched was burning; the shock and pain almost caused him to fall. He negotiated three more rungs and felt one, well and truly ablaze, give way under his weight. A gasp of relief erupted from him as he felt his feet reach the bakery roof and, by then, watchers in the alley were dashing clear and the ladder wholly ablaze. The Texans let go and, as it tumbled downward, turned away from that edge of the roof.

"I guess," Stretch said nervously, "maybe it's time we should think of savin' *our own* necks."

Gathering up the lariat and the thicker rope, Larry glanced westward.

"Other side of the back alley is too far," he observed.

"Well now, I told you we couldn't reach that other roof with the ladder," Stretch reminded him, gesturing to the building on the south side. "South alley's too wide."

"We'd best take a look," decided Larry.

"Well . . . " Stretch shrugged and grimaced. "We got nothin' better to do."

What they saw from the hotel roof's south side was less than encouraging. The Commercial Building accommodated quite a few business offices, the Cattlemen's Association, the Merchants' Co-operative, the County Recorder's Office, the consulting rooms of

Cormack's other doctor, for instance. Also the living quarters of the building's owner and wife. Directly below the Texans, the south wall of the hotel was burning fiercely. Behind them, the hotel roof was crumbling.

"Only one thing we can do," frowned Larry, fashioning a loop in the thicker rope.

"I'd be right obliged if you'd tell me what," muttered Stretch, "on account of I'm gettin' nervous."

"Nervous hell," scoffed Larry. "You ain't no more nervous than I am."

"'Scuse me for mentionin' it," countered Stretch, "But you are lookin' plenty worried."

"Worried — me? Hogwash!" retorted Larry. "Couple more minutes and we'll be safe as if we were squattin' on our blankets, watchin' our horses feedin' on good grass and fixin' ourselves a pot of coffee."

"I'm sure glad to hear that," said Stretch.

"Chimney on that other buildin',"

said Larry, gesturing. "From here, we can rope it easy. Then we swing."

"Uh — we do what?"

"We swing. If we go feet-first, I calculate we could flop on one of them balconies half-way down."

"And likely break our necks."

"Nope. A leg maybe. But it beats going down the other way."

"Meanin' when this ol' roof caves in?"

"Meanin' that. Which rope d'you want to use? Your choice."

"If it's okay by you. I'd as soon take my chances with the lariat."

"You got it. Here we go."

At his second attempt, Larry dropped his noose over the chimney rising up from the roof on the other side of the alley.

"Okay, I get the idea," nodded Stretch. "But I'd be obliged if you'd go first, runt. I want to see how you do it."

"Yeah, sure," nodded Larry, gripping his rope. "'Be seein' you, stringbean."

"I sure hope," Stretch said earnestly.

His scalp crawled as Larry stepped off the roof to begin a wild swing toward the opposite wall, downward at speed, then onward, carried on by the impetus.

7

Track of Five Riders

ABOUT to quit the southside alley, one of the volunteers had glanced upward and sighted the Texans silhouetted at the roof-edge. At his urging, the tarpaulin was stretched again.

"I dunno how they're gonna get down, but we better be ready!"

"Hell, Bob, they're trapped up there!"

"Sure they're trapped — so maybe they'll do somethin' rash."

Larry, when the side wall of the Commercial Building seemed to rush up to meet him, allowed for everything except his formidable weight. His legs were doubled and he was preparing to let go of his rope and grab at anything, a window-ledge, a drainpipe, the rail of a fire-escape, anything at all, when he crashed onto a timber balcony with jarring force.

Nobody had sat on that balcony for a year or more. A flimsy structure at best, weakened by the exposure to the elements, it was no match for such an impact. Before Larry could dive for the window, it was breaking up, collapsing under him; he was falling again.

Accompanied by five pieces of cracked timber, he plunged into the alley, somersaulted and hit the canvas backside-first. His fall was broken and he was unharmed, so it didn't matter that two of the volunteers lost their grip of the tarp; it was still under him when he sprawled flat on his back.

"Lawd Almighty!" he heard a man gasp. "My shoulder's busted!"

There were other casualties. Jagged timber had scored a furrow in the arm of another helper. Another had sprained a wrist and there was more than one dislocated shoulder. They had saved Larry's life, but at some cost.

"I'm sure sorry . . . " he began, as he struggled to his feet. "Listen, fellers, you have the doc tend your hurts and I'll take care of the bill."

"I reckon that's fair," groaned the man with the damaged wrist. "But now we better holler for help. We can't hold that tarp no more — and your buddy's still up there."

"Damn it, he ain't waitin'!" cried the man with the bloody arm. "Look! Now *he's* swingin'!"

Having thrown his loop over that same chimney, and mindful of the flames spurting up through seven openings in the hotel roof, Stretch was imitating the action of his partner. He too swung down and outward, doubling his legs, fervently hoping to drop onto a more substantial balcony or maybe the firestairs, anything but a blank section of wall.

From the alley, seven men stared upward and watched the figure swing pendulum-like from the roof of the doomed hotel to the north wall of the adjoining building — and then nothing. They heard no splintering of timbers, no impact. From down here on the alley floor, they could see nothing.

"Where'd he go?" frowned Larry. "I saw him swing, but . . . "

"Where'd he go?" echoed another man.

Realizing he was headed straight for a window, Stretch had let go of the lariat and covered his face with his arms, anticipating the effects of shattering glass. The window, however, was wide open. He hurtled through it cleanly and flopped on his back, no jarring sensation, no pain. He had fallen onto something soft. He was completely unscathed and grateful to be alive, but also confused. Where was he? It was pitch-dark in here, until . . .

A match flared and a lamp was lit. He drew his arms behind him, blinking against the yellow light. And then his jaw sagged and his eyebrows shot up. He was sprawled on half of a double bed, his head at its bottom end, his feet resting on a pillow. The other half of the bed was occupied by she who had lit the lamp, an overweight, eagerly smiling female. And to his alarm, she was obviously more elated than dismayed by this invasion of her privacy.

"He'll be out there watching the fire," she informed him with an inviting smile. "Then him and his friends will go to some bar to talk and drink, so he won't be back for an hour or more."

"Who — ?" he dared to ask.

"Moriarty — my husband," she cooed. "What's *your* name, dearie?"

"Smith!" he gasped, as he rolled off the bed.

"What's your hurry?" she protested.

On his way to the bedroom door, he mumbled,

"'Scuse me, ma'am! I gotta feed my horse!"

In a bad state of nerves, Stretch hustled out of that room and along a passage, found the stairs and descended to the ground floor. When he reached the street, he spotted his partner, the lawmen and the firefighters retreating to the opposite sidewalk. They had good reason to hurry, and their reason was good enough for him. He hurried after them as the hotel began crumbling.

"Ready with that fire-truck, fellers!" He heard a man yell. "And fetch more buckets! We gotta douse her good — before the bakery or the Commercial catch fire!"

Had there been a strong wind this night, the Penn House might not have been the only casualty. At that, the collapse of the gutted building was an awesome event. In less than a minute, it crumbled to a heap of burning debris. Smoke and sparks invaded the street. Smoldering timbers clattered into Main and the alleys behind and both sides and, at once, the Cormack volunteer firefighters got to work again, cheered on by the enthralled crowd.

When his partner materialized beside him, Larry lost interest in the remains of the Penn House. He expressed his gratitude at Stretch's deliverance and added a question.

"You made it, stringbean. It's sure good to see you alive, but . . . "

"Runt, I got to say I'm as pleased as you."

"But where the hell've you been? I lost sight of you when you hit that wall!"

"I'm plumb thankful you lost sight of me. And I didn't hit no wall."

"What then?"

"Flew clear through an open window — onto a bed."

"Hot damn!" enthused Larry. "You got the craziest luck!"

"You wouldn't say that," winced Stretch, "if you knew what else was in that bed."

"Meanin' what?" demanded Larry.

"Nothin'," sighed Stretch. "I don't want to talk of it."

"It was rough for you, huh?" Larry waxed solicitous. "Left up on that roof all by yourself. Only natural you want to forget it."

"What happened after I swung off of that roof was spookier," declared Stretch. "And *that's* what I want to forget." He changed the subject. "What's that you're totin'?"

"I found our hats, our hardware too," said Larry.

He surrendered his partner's battered Stetson and belted Colts. Automatically, they donned the headgear and strapped on their sidearms before joining Holbrook and his deputy. Old Aaron was warmly thanked and complimented on his skill with the warbow. To this, the veteran cheerfully replied,

"Wasn't no other way of gettin' a line up to you."

"Both doctors are tending burn cases and other casualties," muttered Holbrook. "The miracle is there were no deaths. Except for the night-clerk."

"And it wasn't the fire killed him," growled Larry.

"Doc Edwards inspected the body before they took it away," nodded Holbrook.

"His skull was busted," said Stretch.

"Somethin' else you better know," offered Larry. "When we hustled into the lobby, first thing I smelled was coal-oil."

"Place stunk of coal-oil," Stretch recalled.

"You aren't the first to tell me of that," Holbrook said grimly.

"Some of the boys, them that got here first," nodded Aaron. "They even found the empty cans in the back alley."

"So this fire was no accident," said Holbrook. "And it's obvious the night-clerk was murdered to prevent his identifying the man who started the inside stairs burning."

"I'm still askin' around," muttered Aaron, turning away.

"Stay on it, Aaron," urged Holbrook. When the deputy had disappeared into the crowd, he remarked to the Texans, "It's too early to speculate on a motive. I'll fret about that when I catch up with the arsonists."

"So Aaron's gonna find out . . . ?" began Stretch.

"Right," nodded Holbrook. "If anybody was seen lurking about the hotel. If anybody was sighted leaving town in a hurry. They'd be the obvious suspects." He eyed the tall men perplexedly. "Meanwhile, I'm trying to understand how you survived this mess. I'm told you're responsible for saving a great many lives, including the Penns and the Archands."

"We stayed busy," Larry said off-handedly. "And lucky."

"Lucky is an understatement," said Holbrook. "You were wet to the skin when you barged into the hotel. Now you're bone dry. Damn it, the heat must've been intense."

"It was too hot for comfort," nodded Larry.

"We ain't sayin' we enjoyed ourselves," shrugged Stretch.

Within the hour, old Aaron and his boss had acquired the same information from several different parties. South of the burning hotel and from vantage points all the way to the outskirts of town, five riders had been seen. Strangers they were, but familiar to at least one citizen; he recalled they had stayed at the Brewer House.

When the lawmen hurried to that small hotel, the Texans automatically followed them. In the lobby, they found Brewer in conversation with a bearded man of solemn demeanor.

"A holocaust," Norman was sadly remarking. "Such terrible destruction — so many lives endangered."

"This here's Mister Garth Norman, Sheriff," offered the hotelkeeper. "He's a kind of a reformer, know what I mean?"

Holbrook curtly acknowledged the introduction and got down to cases. Brewer listened to his questions and was ready with an answer.

"Oh, sure. You mean those five cowhands bound for Colorado. They checked out tonight."

"At what time?" demanded Holbrook.

"Right after supper," said Brewer. "Well, they were only here to rest up a few days. Just paid their bill and left."

"Left this hotel," countered Holbrook. "But could've stayed in town quite a time before they rode out." He inspected the register. "Emhardt — two of that name — Kellerman and . . . "

"Ranch-workers," interjected Norman. "On their way to some ranch in Colorado."

"You talked to these men?" frowned Holbrook.

"We passed the time of day," nodded Norman. "In my travels I've met many such men. Just ranch-workers, Sheriff. Cowhands, horse-breakers and such."

Quitting the Brewer House with his deputy and the Texans at his heels, Holbrook announced his intention of pursuing and questioning the south-bound riders.

"Won't take me but a minute to get our animals ready," offered Aaron.

"Do that," urged Holbrook. "I'll be

waiting in the office." To Larry, he remarked, "It may not mean anything, but it's the only lead I have, so I have to follow up on it."

"The way it sounds," drawled Larry, "They didn't stay on to watch the fire."

"Which is what ninety-nine men out of hundred'd do," opined Stretch. "Runt, what d'you say I fetch our horses?"

"Well now," said Larry, "I reckon Kate and the kids'll be safe enough. She won't be lookin' for us till around noon tomorrow."

"You mean noon today." Holbrook checked his watch as Stretch moved off uptown. "It is now ten after one. Sunday morning." He entered his office with Larry tagging, took a bottle from a drawer of his desk and found four glasses. "Valentine, if you and your friend insist on riding with me . . ."

"You don't have to say it," drawled Larry. "Relax, Holbrook. We're just goin' along for the ride. You're in charge."

"It's no time for jumping to conclusions," complained Holbrook. "All I have is witnesses who saw five riders leaving town sometime after the fire began. Nobody saw anybody acting suspiciously in the vicinity of the Penn House. *That's* the kind of witness I need. Unless any of the five was seen with a can of coal-oil, or entering or leaving the hotel, hanging around the side or back alleys, I've got nothing."

"But you're gonna brace 'em anyway, right?" prodded Larry. "Look 'em over? Size 'em up?"

"I should do at least that much," shrugged Holbrook.

When stretch and Aaron arrived, he filled four glasses. Fortified by that one stiff shot of whiskey, the lawmen and the Texans moved out to their horses, got mounted and began their southward journey.

"Anybody ask for us, they'll soon find out what we're about," offered

Aaron, as they cleared the outskirts. "I told Leo and Doc Edwards and a few other fellers."

By 2 a.m., the last Council Valley hands were homebound and Cormack quietening down. The fire had been subdued; the cleaning-up operation was postponed till daylight. In a spare bedroom of their fine home on Teton Avenue, the Archands were going to pains to comfort their guests. At their insistence, the Penns would stay with them until their situation was re-organized. In sleeping attire supplied by their friends, Penn and his wife sat on the edge of the bed and sipped the hot toddies prepared by the sympathetic Jessie. The mayor, his burned hand having been treated by a local doctor, was getting his nerves under control and striving to boost his spirits.

"To be burned out is a nerve-wracking disaster, I know," he said gently. "But surely, old friend, we should all be counting our blessings."

"We four could have died tonight," frowned his wife. "It's a frightening thought, and I suppose we'd prefer to thrust it from our minds . . . "

"As if we could ever forget," sighed Albertina. "On that roof — waiting for it to happen — was just terrifying."

"So let's not try to forget," suggested Jessie. "Cleave's right. We're lucky to be alive and should count our blessings. You've suffered a heavy loss, Emory dear, but you know Cleave and I will help any way we can."

"Your hospitality is much appreciated, Jessie," nodded Penn. He took his wife's hand and worked up a comforting smile. "It's not the end of the world, my dear."

"Just the end of the Penn House — the finest in Cormack," sniffed Albertina.

"You'll recall I took time to empty our safe before we climbed to the roof," he said. "It contained only a couple of hundred dollars, but every little helps. And, of course, we still have our savings, every dollar secure in the safe at the Reliance. We'll rebuild, Tina. The new Penn House will have to be a small building unfortunately, but at least I'll be in business again and you'll be properly provided for," He grinned encouragingly, "as befits one of Cormack's finest ladies."

"You girls were an inspiration tonight," declared Archand. "You agree, Emory?"

"An inspiration," nodded Penn. "And to think they're called the weaker sex."

"Both of them braver than they realize," enthused the mayor.

"I was praying for a miracle," confided Jessie. "And then, to my astonishment, those begrimed giants came climbing out of the manhole! Who on earth *were* they?"

"Two very rough characters," offered her husband. "Since their arrival in our town, they've been involved in two violent brawls and a shooting affray."

"Not exactly two of our kind,"

remarked Penn. "Yet we owe them so much."

"We'll look for them later, Emory," suggested Archand, "and convey our gratitude."

"But that can wait" Jessie said briskly. "We all need our sleep."

"I'm just exhausted," sighed Albertina.

"We'll leave you now," announced Archand, taking his wife's arm. "Until breakfast, my friends. And we'll make it a late breakfast."

★ ★ ★

At intervals during the pre-dawn hours Stretch and the old scout dismounted to fashion torches of brush tied to sapling rods and, by their light, study sign on the south trail. Always the same reading. The five were still pressing south.

"How far to the south border of Bridger County?" demanded Holbrook, when they resumed the pursuit.

"The way they're moseyin' along,

Breck boy," drawled Aaron, "we'll be out of the county 'fore sun-up. And it ain't likely we'll find these Emhardts and their buddies meantime."

In dawn's first light they easily located the Emhardt camp. Track of the five riders drew them off the regular trail and across 50 yards of brushy terrain to the west, then into the stand of timber above which the campfire smoke was visible. Deep within the timbers, the Emhardts and their cohorts were camped by a spring. They showed no tension. The men hunkered by the fire raised thier eyes from the sizzling pans and the steaming coffeepot and nodded a welcome. The one stripped down to his underwear, washing his outer garments in the spring, offered a howdy and went on with his chore.

After his first appraisal of this rough-looking quintet, Holbrook chose to stay mounted during the interrogation. Aaron and the Texans took their cue and did likewise.

Dex Emhardt nodded sadly in

response to the lawman's questions.

"You're dead right, Sheriff. We quit town right after the fire started."

"You had checked out of the Brewer House early last night," said Holbrook.

"Well, sure," grunted the man knee-deep in the spring. "Right after supper, as I recall."

"Then we hung around the saloons," drawled Burt Emhardt. "Figured to warm the inner man, as they say, before we lit out for Colorado."

"When that fire started — hell!" The elder brother shook his head mournfully. "I'll tell you, Sheriff, brother Burt and me couldn't bear to stay and watch. We got too many bad memories."

"Is that so?" prodded Holbrook.

"That's how our old man died," sighed Dex.

"Our Uncle Dade too," nodded Burt.

"Hotel fire in Montana," muttered Dex. "That was a long time back, you know? But a man never forgets. And, ever since, we've carried this sadness inside of us."

"And a bad feelin' about — uh — places that catch fire — with folks trapped inside," said Burt, grimacing. "No way we could join the crowd and watch such a fire. We just ain't got the heart for it."

Holbrook threw out a few more questions, only to draw a blank. None of the five could help him in his investigation. They had been two blocks away when the hotel caught fire. They had seen nobody carrying coal-oil.

"All right, that's it." He nodded to Aaron. "We'd best return to town."

In silence, the lawmen and the Texans rode out of the clearing, through the trees and back across the brushy area to the regular trail. They had traveled 100 yards of the return journey to Cormack before Larry called a halt and said his piece.

"We're out of your territory, so it ain't no use you objectin'," he told the sheriff. "Mind now, we ain't on the prod, my partner and me. It's just I'm still curious about those Colorado-bound hombres."

"I believe I asked all the necessary questions," Holbrook said sternly.

"*I* got questions," retorted Larry.

"You leery of them jaspers, Larry boy?" asked Aaron.

"Ever had a feelin' in your bones, old timer?" prodded Larry.

"At my age, all the goldurned time," grouched Aaron. "Dang-blasted rheumatics."

"With me, it's somethin' else," said Larry.

"Valentine, I have to get back to the county seat," said Holbrook. "And you're right. I have no authority here, so you and Emerson are free to do as you wish. But do you mind telling me why you're dissatisfied with their explanation?"

"It's just a hunch," said Larry. "I'll tell you about it next time I see you." He nodded to Stretch. "Let's go."

At that bend of the trail, the two investigators, two official, two freelance, parted company and went their separate ways, Holbrook and his deputy making for Cormack, the Texans riding 50 yards south, then quitting the trail to begin a cautious advance on the timber.

"You gonna tell me why we're doin' this?" enquired Stretch.

"Kind of early for a hombre to wash his duds," remarked Larry.

The taller Texan whistled softly.

"Mighty early. So — uh — he'd have a special reason."

"How d'you like this for a special reason?" offered Larry. "They had to be seen quittin' town. They maybe counted on somebody followin' 'em and askin' questions. Suppose now one of 'em got oil on his clothes while he was dousin' the hotel walls? That'd be a dead giveaway."

"Ain't that the truth," agreed Stretch. "You think that's what happened?"

"All I'm sayin' is I caught a whiff

of somethin'," said Larry. "And I was closest to the lard-bellied hombre in the pool."

"And what you sniffed could've been coal-oil?" frowned Stretch.

"Sure wasn't bay rum," growled Larry. "Cool your saddle. From here on, we travel on our bellies."

Shielded by one of the thicker brush-clumps, the sorrel and pinto were left ground-hobbled. The trouble-shooters then went to ground and began crawling until they reached the timber. Moving from tree to tree, they warily advanced to within earshot of the camp.

The voices were gruff, subdued, but audible. Kellerman, the portly one, was out of the pool and hanging his clothes to dry.

"All the way to Quiller's Ford — to wait for 'em?" he growled at the brothers. "Listen, Quiller's Ford is quite a trace from here. You all that sure we'll ever see 'em again?"

"Toddy got a point, Dex," remarked

Burt Emhardt. "We only got their word for it. And we don't know Norman real good."

"Cal Fulbright vowed we could trust him, but I dunno," frowned the elder brother. "All that bank cash, that's a lot of temptation."

"A thousand per man they promised us," another of the five reminded him. "That's five thousand extra for Norman and Fulbright if they just forget about us."

"If, instead of hangin' around Cormack a while and then headin' south to the Ford, they just take off north or east," said Kellerman. "Hell, Dex, we handled all the big chores, didn't we?"

"That was the deal," shrugged Dex. "We keep the whole town clear of the bank by settin' the Penn House afire, so nobody cares what's happenin' way downtown." He frowned impatiently and rubbed at his belly. "That grub near ready, Steve?"

"Never mind the grub," muttered

his brother. "Do we head back to Cormack or go on to Quiller's Ford — and maybe never see 'em again?"

"I'm thinkin' on it," said Dex.

Having heard enough — more than enough — the Texans might have waited a while, choosing their own time for challenging the arsonists. The first move was made by Kellerman, however, when he moved into the timber with the idea of answering a call of nature. He came in so quickly that, before the eavesdroppers could change position, he was in arm's length of Stretch. Inclined to prompt action on such occasions, the taller Texan swung his bunched left fast and hard and, with the impact of a mule's kick, the blow struck Kellerman's right ear. As his legs buckled, Stretch caught him to lower him gently to the ground. Larry then shrugged resignedly, crooked a finger and stepped clear of his tree.

Side by side the tall men emerged from the timber to confront the startled four at a distance of some 18 feet.

The other two were quick to follow the example of the brothers, who leapt to their feet.

"Just what the hell's the idea of . . . ?" began Dex Emhardt.

"You've been shootin' off your mouths," Larry said coldly.

"And we've been listenin'," drawled Stretch.

"So do I have to spell it out for you?" challenged Larry. "We're takin' you back to Cormack alive — 'less some fool tries throwin' down on us."

"The hell you are," retorted Burt Emhardt, his eyes narrowing. "How do we know the sheriff and his over-the-hill deputy are backin' your play?"

"They ain't," shrugged Stretch. "They're quite a ways from here. Headed back to town."

"Your skinny sidekick's kinda loose-mouthed, hero," the elder brother jeered at Larry. "Now we know there's only the two of you!"

"Uh huh," grunted Larry. "And only four of you."

224

He meant that as a warning, but nobody heeded it. As the Emhardt's hands flashed to their holsters, the other two began drawing, Larry sidestepped and filled his hand and Stretch's matched Colts were out and roaring.

Both brothers hurtled backward to collapse and writhe and then Larry's gun roared almost in unison with the rogue drawing a bead on him. The man yelled wildly and, off-balance from the impact of Larry's bullet, spun and flopped into the pool. The fourth man, covered by three leveled Colts, promptly lost his courage and his grip of his weapon. It slid from his grasp. His hands shot up as he gasped a plea,

"Don't shoot!"

"I won't," scowled Larry, "'long as you stay froze."

"While you're coverin' these no-accounts, I'll hogtie the fat one," offered Stretch.

What needed to be done was done quickly. The unscathed quitter was ordered to help his wounded cohort out of the spring while Larry checked on the Emhardt brothers and collected guns. Not for the first time, Stretch had proved his deadly accuracy with either hand.

"That makes it two dead, one wounded, one sore-headed and one healthy and talkative," Larry reported, when his partner toted Kellerman to the campfire. He unhitched a lariat and tossed it, then stared hard at the undamaged survivor. "You got a name?"

"Gillane," the man replied.

"Know what I mean by talkative?" prodded Larry. "You try keepin' your mouth shut 'tween here and the Cormack calaboose, you'll be the sorest polecoat ever got dumped in a cell."

"I know when I'm licked," mumbled Gillane, his shoulders slumped in defeat. "Toddy was likely right. Fulbright and that other jasper would've double-crossed us — so I'll tell you anything you want to know."

In Cormack, meanwhile, a citizen of tender years, nine-year-old Herbie Walker, was hunting his lost dog. Answering to the name Amos, that adventurous mongrel had disappeared after scuttling under the Meldrum Reliance Bank.

Later, when Holbrook and his deputy rode in, they found five leading citizens awaiting them on the law office porch. The Archands were dressed for Sunday services, the haggard Emory Penn and his wife garbed in clothing loaned by their host and hostess. The fifth citizen looked to be on the verge of a nervous breakdown. He was slight of physique and sharp-featured and, right now, his complexion was pasty grey.

His name was Chester Meldrum.

8

Hate is a Deadly Master

AS the lawmen dismounted, Archand called urgently to Holbrook.

"Unlock your door and take us inside, Breck. We have to keep this quiet for as long as possible."

"It *can't* be a secret!" gasped the banker. "The Walker boy is bound to tell his parents — and they'll talk. And don't forget the bartender who helped rescue the dog. Bartenders are as blabber-mouthed as barbers!"

"In an hour or less, the other victims will know," Penn said shakily.

After Holbrook had ushered the party into his office, old Aaron hustled to provide extra seating. He needn't have troubled himself; Penn and the banker were too agitated to get off their feet. The women sat on the office couch, holding hands, Albertina weeping softly.

"Breck, where have you been?" frowned Archand. "Not that it would've made any difference, but . . . "

"I passed the word around, Mister Mayor," offered Aaron. "Five strangers quit town right after the fire started."

"Naturally I had to find them and interrogate them," said Holbrook.

"You have to *do* something — and *quickly*!" insisted Meldrum.

"Steady, Chet," chided Archand. "Better let me explain."

He dealt it out for the lawmen in a few short sentences. Finding your Herbie Walker in the alley beside the bank, fretting over the inexplicable disappearance of his pet, barkeep Jerry Ness had taken pity on the boy and offered to help. Herbie insisted the mongrel had ventured under the bank but had not emerged from the other side nor from the front or rear. Investigating, Ness had found the animal inside the bank, also his means of entry, a jagged gap in the floor; all Amos had to do was scamper up a down-hanging floorboard.

"You can guess the rest," said Archand. "Ness sent the boy home and hurried straight to Chet's home. Unfortunately, Ness isn't the only one who saw the open safe. The Walker boy climbed in after him."

"And you can bet your Sunday high hat Jerry said, 'Looka there! The safe's been looted!'" drawled Aaron. "That kind of bad news gonna travel fast through this here town."

Out of deference to the ladies, Holbrook resisted the urge to swear. He clamped a cigar between his teeth as he gave bent to his chagrin.

"So now we know why Mister Penn's hotel was set afire. The bank-robbers needed a distraction, and the arsonists certainly provided it!

"All my clients will be ruined!" groaned Meldrum. "Don't just sit there, Sheriff Holbrook! Surely every minute counts!"

"Keep your shirt on, Mister Banker-man," frowned Aaron. "Sheriff and me ain't had no sleep since we opened our eyes yesterday mornin', but we'll get to workin' on this deviltry rightaway."

"Everybody ruined?" challenged Holbrook. "Mister Meldrum, are you saying you have no insurance?"

"Can you imagine how I feel — having to admit that?" cried Meldrum. He gesticulated wildly. "Emory here, he'll be one of the biggest losers! Neither of us believed in insurance — until now!"

"As of this moment, Sheriff, I have only two hundred and eighty dollars, give or take a dollar or two," muttered Penn. "Unless the bank's funds are recovered, I'm wiped out. My wife and I don't even own the clothes on our backs."

"If this sheriff were as much a detective as he is a gunman, there'd be *some* hope!" hissed Jessie.

231

"That's enough," her husband sharply chided her. "I'm confident our sheriff will do his utmost to apprehend the thieves and retrieve the stolen money."

"Thank you, Mayor Archand," said Holbrook. "And now, if you good people will kindly excuse us, my deputy and I will get started on our investigation."

"Oh, Lord!" groaned Albertina. "How I wish you *were* an investigator, instead of . . . !"

"A gunfighter with a badge, Mrs Penn?" challenged Holbrook, his eyes gleaming. "A hireling unfit to cross the thresholds of the better homes of this community?"

"Sheriff, my wife is over-wrought," protested Penn. He went to the couch to take Albertina's arms. "I think enough has been said. Cleave — Chet — we should leave now."

After the civic leaders had gone their way, old Aaron stifled a yawn and eyed his chief expectantly.

"How about I boil up some coffee?"

"I need coffee the way I need to keep on breathing, but you know better," muttered Holbrook, reaching for his hat. "We just don't have time, Aaron."

"I guess we start by checkin' the hotels," shrugged Aaron.

"Anybody who has left town," nodded Holbrook. "Transients, locals, anybody at all. Oh, hell, I could use a *dozen* deputies now!" As he moved out of the office, he gestured wearily. "Start at the north end of Main, Aaron, while I take the hotels and doss-houses at the south end."

Soon enough, the sheriff's search brought him to the small hotel opposite his office. If not an actual atheist, Brewer was no churchman; he was sweeping his lobby when Holbrook walked in on him.

"'Morning," he nodded. "Black Sunday for Cormack, huh Sheriff? I'm sure thankful my extra cash is in the Cattlemen's Trust Bank. Now, if I was one of Mister Meldrum's clients . . . "

"It doesn't take long at all, does it?" scowled Holbrook. "Nothing travels faster than a bullet — or bad news. Now pay attention, because this is important. I know of five of your guests who checked out since the fire. Were there any others?"

"No, only those ranch-hands headed for Colorado," said Brewer. "Mister Norman rode out a little while ago, but . . . "

"Who?"

"Norman. You met him here, remember? Tall gent with the whiskers — here to reform all the sinners hereabouts? When I saw him ride out, I got that old feeling, you know?"

"Quitting town without paying the rent on his room."

"I'm ashamed for being so suspicious, but it happens all the time." Brewer grinned wryly. "Well, I needn't have fretted about Mister Norman. Used my pass-key to check his room. His stuff is still there and no sign of him packing.

So he'll be back. Just taking a ride, I guess."

Glancing uptown after he emerged from the Brewer House, Holbrook at once assumed his deputy had news for him. Old Aaron was headed his way, his movements urgent. But then Aaron pointed excitedly and Holbrook turned to stare southward. Small wonder his deputy was hustling.

The Texans were back, and not exactly empty-handed. From the south edge of town, they ambled their mounts toward the law office, Larry leading the horses toting the tied-down bodies of the Emhardt brothers, Stretch in charge of the animals straddled by the three live prisoners, one unscathed, one with a shoulder wound, one with a headache that wouldn't quit.

"Valentine and his hunches," muttered Holbrook, as Aaron intercepted him while crossing the street.

"You got to hand it to them bucks, son," chuckled Aaron. "Just full of surprises, ain't they?"

They unlocked and opened the office. Staying mounted, Larry asked directions to the funeral parlor.

"Save us some time," he offered. "While I'm unloading these stiffs, Stretch can tell you what we learned from the live ones."

By the time he returned from the funeral parlor and dismounted at the law office hitch-rail, the over-worked and disgruntled Dr Maurice Edwards was administering to Kellerman and the other injured man in a cell. Installed in the adjoining cell, the only unhurt survivor, desperate for leniency, was offering his statement. In the passage, Holbrook was using Stretch's back as a desk, writing busily, committing the statement to paper. Aaron aimed an aimable grin at Larry as he entered the passage.

Larry paused then to study another survivor, the still unidentified left-over from the gunfight at Sharney's bar.

"You look interested," he accused. "And plenty sore."

"Damn Norman anyway," Garrett said impulsively.

"Keep talkin'," invited Larry.

"The hell with you," sneered Garrett. "I got nothin' to say."

"He said Norman's name," Larry remarked to Holbrook. "You think Norman was about to reform him? When hell freezes over."

"Some jackpot you've handed me," growled Holbrook. He passed pad and pencil through the bars. "Gillane's your name you say? All right, Gillane. Read the statement, then sign it. Aaron, you know what to do."

"Uh huh," nodded Aaron. "The peddler-man's maybe still around — and you'll want to know where."

The deputy hurried out, leaving his chief to acknowledge his debt to the Texans.

"So much you've accomplished," declared Holbrook. "And in such a short time. Wherever they're headed, Norman and Fulbright will still be in reach. So I may yet recover the stolen cash — thanks to you two."

"I got me a thought about that," drawled Larry, crooking a finger. "You got a minute? Time for a pow-wow."

Gillane signed and returned the pad. Holbrook took it from him and followed the tall men along to the connecting doorway.

"I'm in your debt, Valentine," he muttered. "But now I'm reminding you I'm entitled to an explanation. Why *were* you suspicious of the Emhardt bunch?"

"Man don't wash his duds so early in the mornin' 'less he's got a good reason," shrugged Larry. "Kellerman's reason was a dead giveaway. Coal-oil, Holbrook. I caught a whiff of it. So now you know why we sneaked back."

"Pays to play it sneaky," Stretch remarked with a mild grin. "When we got to snoopin', they were chewin' the fat. So we just naturally learned a thing or two."

"Listen now, Holbrook, about that

bank loot," frowned Larry. "Chances are it's stashed in Fulbright's wagon."

"Logical assumption," nodded Holbrook.

"Sure, and somethin' you'd better know about us," said Larry. "We'll side you, but we don't want any credit for whatever we do, savvy?"

"Don't need it," Stretch assured the lawman. "No matter how we handle it . . ."

"It's got to be you fetches the dinero back to Cormack," insisted Larry. "Got to be you turns it in."

"Neater that way," drawled Stretch. "Hell, that's what they're payin' you for."

"A little while ago, Chester Meldrum bent my ear," Holbrook grimly recalled. "The man was distraught — and showing little faith in my ability. Yes, by Godfrey, I might take you up on that offer, Valentine, but not because I crave glory. Hell, no. I only want to see the expression on Meldrum's face."

"Him and all the high-falutin' citizens

— eatin' crow," grinned Larry. "A lawman is somethin' better'n a badge-totin' gunslinger, right?"

"Somebody's been talking," said Holbrook, eyeing him warily. "Seems to me you've learned a lot about Cormack's attitude toward me — and vice versa."

The awkward moment was cut short by the return of old Aaron, who reported,

"Peddler's camped just a mile along the west trail. I just talked to a feller bought a new hat off of him yesterday."

"From that wagon, I hope to take something of greater value than a new hat," Holbrook said briskly. "We'll see you later, Aaron. You're in charge till I get back."

So quickly did the sheriff move, the Texans had to hustle to keep up with him. Through the office and into the street they hurried to slip their reins and step up to leather. At a hard gallop, they rode out of Cormack and onto the west trail.

Some time later, with Fulbright's camp in sight, Larry wrestled with a thought he chose to keep to himself. He had been only too willing to ally himself to this territory's unappreciated boss-lawman, but now he was wishing Holbrook had taken time to plan a strategy instead of riding in bull-headed. Their advance must have been audible to Fulbright for the past several minutes and their dust clearly visible.

Only the one man, Fulbright, was hunkered by the campfire. The picketed team kept their heads down, feeding. The wagon was a colorful sight in the morning sun. No saddle-horse to be seen. No sign of another man.

Fulbright rose to greet them as they reined up in a flurry of dust.

"Well, Sheriff, we meet again." He nodded affably. "I trust I've camped the approved distance from the town limits? You're here on business, I hope? Listen, I can show you a fine line of shirts, cravats, headgear . . . "

"This is business, make no mistake

about that," Holbrook coldly informed him. "But *law* business, Fulbright. I'm here to arrest you for bank robbery."

"For what?" blinked Fulbright. "Hey, is this some kind of joke?"

"Nobody's laughin', mister," warned Stretch. "Specially the losers in the calaboose."

"Their names will be familiar to you," scowled Holbrook. "Gillane, Kellerman and Ross."

"The one called Gillane talked up a storm," drawled Larry. "The Emhardt boys, they ain't talkin' at all. They're grave-bait."

"I know it all, Fulbright," declared Holbrook.

"Is that so? Well, you know more than *I* know." Fulbright resorted to bluster. "I don't care what you've been told. I never heard of the men you're speaking of and I sure haven't robbed any bank."

"Why waste our time?" challenged Holbrook. "Fulbright, it's just too late for a bluff-play."

"You're talking to an innocent man," asserted Fulbright. "What're you after? Stolen money?" He gestured to the wagon. "Search my rig. Go on, I dare you. If you can find one dollar of stolen bank cash in there, it'll be a miracle!"

Holbrook was about to dismount when Larry sharply chided him.

"Don't bother, Holbrook. D'you think he'd say what he said — if the cash was stashed in the wagon?"

As he spoke, he dropped his gaze to the ground and, too late, noted the hoofprints of one horse leading into the brush to his left. Just this once, he was taken off-guard. From somewhere in that screening brush a pistol barked thrice, and Fulbright was quick to take advantage. Holbrook's mount, its rump bullet-burned, reared startled, throwing him. He fell against Larry with heavy impact, drove him off-balance and, as they went to ground with the lawman uppermost, Fulbright drew from his shoulder-holster and cut loose at Stretch. With an oath and a grunt of pain, the taller Texan parted company with his pinto, crashing to the dust with blood streaking his right side, but not inert. He rolled as Fulbright fired again, emptied his leftside holster and fired once from ground level. Fulbright yelled and lurched drunkenly, tried to raise his pistol again, then stumbled forward, dying on his feet, collapsing into the campfire.

To Larry's chagrin, the sheriff's animal was still rearing and kicking, charging around the campsite, still crazed with pain. A flailing hoof missed his head by inches as he began helping Holbrook upright, and then the animal bolted from the scene and his chagrin increased. With the departure of the runaway, he now heard the other hoofbeats, but distant. Beyond a line of rocks, he saw the bearded rider heading eastward at speed, two bulky valises tied to his saddle.

"Of all the lousy luck," he raged, as he let go of the sheriff and hurried across to his prone and groaning partner. "What d'you say, stringbean? How bad . . . ?"

"Well — I'll tell you, runt . . . !" Stretch raised himself to a squatting posture, face contorted, teeth clenched. "No slug in me, but I'm leakin' copious from this here crease. Don't feel like I'll be — helpin' you chase that other sonofabitch."

Holbrook cursed explosively, stepped to the fire and, with a boot, shoved the body clear of it.

"Valentine . . . ?"

"The other one — he'll be Norman — took off eastward," growled Larry.

"I saw him," nodded Holbrook.

"See what's hitched to his cayuse?" challenged Larry.

"Damn right," Holbrook said tersely. "The cash from the Meldrum bank, nothing surer."

"Safe guess," said Larry.

"We have to stay after him!" raged Holbrook. "But — damn it — where's my horse?"

"Straddle mine," offered Stretch. "I sure can't."

"I'll be ridin' with you, Holbrook, But not till I've doctored Stretch," said Larry.

"Don't worry about . . . " began Stretch.

"Hogwash," growled Larry. "I should leave you to flop and bleed? No chance!"

"Valentine, don't think of abandoning your partner — the condition he's in," called Holbrook, as he hurried to mount the pinto. "Do what you can for him. I'll stay with Norman."

"Get goin'," urged Larry. "I'll catch up." As Holbrook rode off, a harrowing thought occurred to him. "Aw, hell! which saddlebag's our bottle in — yours or mine?"

Stretch, who never lost track of their whiskey supply, grinned weakly and nodded to the sorrel. Larry dashed to it, snatched the bottle from his saddlebag and pulled the cork. A stiff shot was fed to his partner, after which he downed a couple of much-needed mouthfuls and hurried to the wagon to rummage for material with which to improvise a dressing and bandages.

As well as boosting Stretch's morale, rye whiskey sterilized the angry gash at his ribs. With the bleeding staunched, Larry makeshifted a dressing and secured it with great care. Stretch was still conscious, but not fooling himself or his partner; they were never less than realistic.

"You won't be ridin' today — any place," Larry warned.

"Ain't that the truth," grunted Stretch. "Feel like a damn fool, runt, lettin' that bastard sneak-draw on me."

"I could tote you to the wagon," offered Larry. "Be more comfortable for you."

"Nope," grunted Stretch. "You'll be comin' back, and right here's where you'll find me. Only other thing you can do for me is — leave that bottle with me — gimme somethin' to hold onto."

"You got it, amigo," sighed Larry, nudging the bottle closer.

"All right now, you better vamoose," urged Stretch. "That badge-toter could be needin' you already. You notice he's some unlucky with horses? His critter near threw a shoe a few days back. This time, it got bullet-burned and threw *him*."

"'Be seein' you," said Larry rising. "Rest easy, beanpole."

"Well, sure," nodded Stretch. "Got nothin' better to do."

With his blood up, Larry remounted the sorrel and heeled it to a run. Eastward he headed, giving his mount full rein, probing the area ahead for his first glimpse of the lawman on Stretch's pinto.

He was on a well-marked trail when disquiet assailed him. The terrain through which he now rode appeared familiar, and for good reason; this route led to Wolf Creek. More cause for alarm a quarter-hour later when he sighted Holbrook. Beside the trail, the lawman was shakily regaining his feet, the pinto standing by, trembling.

"What the hell . . . ?" demanded Larry.

"I don't blame — Emersons's animal . . . " panted Holbrook, as Larry brought the sorrel to a halt. "The best of them will take fright — when that happens." Larry now noted the sheriff's right hand was gun-filled. Holstering the weapon, he gestured irritably. "Other side of the trail. Damned if a rattlesnake didn't slither out of those rocks. Startled the pinto. He bucked and . . . "

"And threw you," growled Larry.

"As if you couldn't guess," grouched Holbrook. "Here, boy." He trudged to the pinto and raised boot to stirrup. "I had the satisfaction of killing the sidewinder with one shot. But, damn the luck, we're losing *time*!"

"If you aim to stay with me — hustle," urged Larry. "In case you ain't noticed, Norman's tracks lead straight to the Preston spread."

For Kate Preston, the nightmare began when the strange rider was heard crossing her west quarter at speed. She was relaxing on the shaded porch of the ranch-house with a bowl in her lap, scraping carrots, watching her son play Indian in the front yard. Irma, a keen student nowadays, was in the parlor with her schoolbooks. At first assuming her tall protectors were returning from last night's visit to Cormack, she suddenly realized only one horseman was headed this way.

The black-garbed, heavily-bearded stranger then arrived, charging his animal into the yard, snarling orders.

"Stay right where you are, woman! You, boy!" He dropped from his panting mount, drew his pistol and glowered at Jarvis and, to Kate's horror, the boy obeyed Norman's command and approached him gingerly. "*Faster*, boy!"

"In heaven's name, what . . . ?" began Kate.

"Silence!" raged Norman. "Boy,

come stand by my horse and hold the rein!" Well and truly intimidated, Jarvis edged past him to take the rein. "Now you stand there, understand? You don't budge!"

"No . . . !" gasped Kate.

"One more word out of you — and the brat's blood is on your head," warned Norman. He stood with his eyes turned to the western approaches, but with the pistol, cocked, leveled at her son. "Obey my orders and no arguments. I'm buying time, woman. When I resume my journey, there'll be no heroes pursuing me. I'll not be chased like a cheap thief!"

Irma emerged from the house and, sighting Norman, the gun and her brother, would have hurried down from the porch had Kate not risen to intercept her. The bowl, knife and carrots fell to the porch. Cradling her daughter in her arms, Kate strove in vain to calm her.

"Quiet, honey! You *must* be quiet — *please* . . . !"

"Run, Jarvis!" cried Irma.

"Shut your mouth," snapped Norman. "The boy knows better."

The tension, nerve-wracking, seemed to last an eternity. There was no movement until, from the west, Norman heard the hoofbeats. He then commanded Kate to leave her daughter on the porch, descent to the yard and walk to the west side of the house.

"I want them to see you. You will beckon them — urgently — do you understand? You're to signal them to come on. And then you will return to that porch. *Do it!*"

Moving clear of the sobbing Irma, Kate quit the porch and walked to the west side. She was in clear view when she signaled them, but Norman, his horse and his tiny hostage obscured by that end of the main building.

"Kate callin' us in," observed Larry.

"And — I get the impression she's in distress," frowned Holbrook. "We have to hurry, Valentine!"

Her nerves a'clamor, Kate retraced

her steps to the porch and stood in front of her daughter with the vague notion of blocking her view of whatever was to follow.

Into the yard rode the lawman and the hard-eyed man on the sorrel and, quickly, Norman swung his gun, fired once and again aimed the weapon at the bug-eyed Jarvis. His face contorted in agony, right arm bloody and useless, Holbrook toppled from the pinto.

"Hidin' behind a woman's skirts is low enough!" raged Larry, as he swung down to confront Norman at a distance of 15 yards. "But — usin' a scared kid . . . !"

"He says he's buying time, Larry!" cried Kate.

"The next thing you'll do is unstrap your gun and throw it into the well," Norman coldly ordered Larry.

"Uh huh." Larry shook his head. "That's the *last* thing I'd do."

"You aren't seeing clearly?" challenged Norman. "I have a bead on the boy. I need only squeeze trigger and his life is snuffed out. And that's what I'll do, unless you . . . "

"You won't kill the kid," countered Larry. "That'd be the end for you, Norman."

"What . . . ?" began Norman.

"Think about it," invited Larry. "The odds are against you."

"Are you blind?" jibed Norman.

"I see real clear," Larry grimly assured him. "You got a bead on the kid sure. And you could kill him — easily. But you'd be next. To take a shot at me, you'd have to re-cock and aim my way. And, while you're doin' that, I'll be drawin' on you."

"No man is that fast," sneered Norman.

"Don't bet your life on it," growled Larry. "Your iron's cocked. Only one way you'll stop me. You'll have to swing it on me — right now — and trigger *muy pronto*."

From the porch, Kate watched both men in an agony of apprehension. From where he lay, plagued by pain,

Holbrook furtively moved his left hand, closing it over a rock about the size of his palm. When he summoned the effort to hurl it, Norman was his intended target. He meant to distract the bearded man and give Larry time to draw and fire, but his aim was erratic.

The rock struck Jarvis' bare foot. The boy promptly yelped and began hopping on his other foot and Larry could wait no longer. He was drawing and cocking when, in frantic haste, Norman swung his gun toward him. The Colt boomed first and Norman seemed to leap backwards, arms flailing, chest bloody. His pistol discharged to the sky and then he was crashing on his back with legs spread and eyes wide open, but unseeing.

Still hopping, loudly complaining the sheriff had thrown a rock at him, Jarvis made it to the porch and his mother's waiting arms. Larry, chilled to his belly, but sweating too, cursed under his breath, holstered his Colt and trudged to where Holbrook lay.

"I didn't — believe you could — do it," mumbled the lawman. "That's why I — had to . . . "

"*Quien sabe?*" shrugged Larry, dropping to one knee. "Maybe I could've. It's somethin' we'll never know, Holbrook. Listen, the arm looks bad."

"Broken, I think," groaned Holbrook.

"You carry him right inside, Larry," called Kate. She had ordered her children into the house and was about to descend from the porch. "We'll put him in my bed and I'll dress his wound and take good care of him for as long as . . . "

"Hell — *no!*" gasped Holbrook. "Not *that!*"

"A real kindly thought, Kate, but forget it," said Larry. "Just hustle up whatever medical stuff you got. We'll clean his arm as best we can, and then I'll have to take him to Cormack. Slug's still in there. A lot of splintered bone and torn muscle. Home doctorin' won't

256

do it. He needs a regular professional."

While she hurried to obey, he walked across to the animal Garth Norman would never ride again and investigated the two valises. He was re-securing them when Kate reappeared. Her curiosity aroused, she demanded to be told,

"What's in the bags?"

Larry shrugged fatalistically.

"Some men're born with it," he muttered. "Some work for it. Some gamble and get it. And some sonsabitches kill for it." As he started back toward Holbrook, he remembered his manners. "Sorry, Kate. Pardon my language."

"You should apologize?" she countered, flicking a scathing glance to the sprawled body. Her next words were mouthed deliberately and, under the circumstances, did not seem outlandish to him. "That bastard *was* a sonofabitch."

"What did she — say . . . ?" gasped Holbrook.

"Nothin' that ain't true," grinned Larry.

★ ★ ★

The return of the sheriff and the Texans was watched by many a gaping local that afternoon. Larry and his weak but still conscious partner shared the seat of the peddler's wagon. In back, Larry had dumped the bodies of Garth Norman and Calvin Fulbright. The sorrel and pinto and the sheriff's retrieved mount were tied to the tailgate. At Larry's insistence, Breck Holbrook, even weaker than Stretch and in greater pain, was astride the animal once ridden by Norman.

"Lost your voice, Sheriff?" the townfolk heard Larry ask, when they drew abreast of the Reliance Bank. "You got somethin' to say, right?"

Holbrook drew rein, coughed to clear his throat and called a request.

"Will somebody — kindly summon Mister Meldrum? And tell him to fetch his keys, please. The bank's cash has been recovered."

Doggedly, Holbrook clung to consciousness for as long as it took the banker to arrive on the scene. He surrendered the tight-packed valises with courtesy and dignity, ignoring Meldrum's fervent speech of gratitude and did not pass out until, a short time later, Larry lifted him onto the table in Doc Edwards' surgery.

Around sundown, perched on the rail of the law office porch, Larry glanced along Main and, with a knowing grin, reported,

"Here she comes."

Slumped in a cane back chair, feeling better for two substantial meals and the ministrations of a local doctor, Stretch worked up an answering grin.

"Herself?"

"Uh huh," nodded Larry. "And the kids. In the buckboard."

As the rig rolled to a halt in front of the county jail, old Aaron emerged to welcome the family. Kate flashed the Texans a warm smile and put her request to the deputy. Would he mind keeping an eye on Irma and Jarvis a while, maybe for an hour?

"Well, howdy there, you young'uns!" beamed Aaron. "How about I arrest you and stash you in a cell till your ma comes for you? That'd be fun, huh?"

"By golly!" enthused Jarvis, climbing down with his sister. "I'll be the youngest kid in Cormack ever got arrested!"

"We can't be arrested," sniffed Irma, as they ascended to the porch. "Only grown-up folks get arrested."

"I guess this just ain't your day, Jarvis," chuckled Stretch.

"You see, I have to visit the sheriff," Kate explained. "Does he still live at . . . ?"

"Yup," nodded Aaron. "Same place. Hey, what'd you fetch him?"

"Supper," she smiled. "They'll warm it up for me at Kiley's Cafe."

"Way to a man's heart, huh?" suggested Larry.

"None of your business," she countered.

"Don't be worryin' about the young 'uns," offered Aaron. "We got no pitcher-books, but I'll let the little missy read all the handbills on wanted killers and such. And the boy can watch me feed the prisoners. They'll have a real good time."

Some twenty minutes later, bedded down in his room at the Gilmeyer Hotel, Breck Holbrook opened his eyes and cocked an ear to a gentle rapping at his door. From shoulder to wrist, his right arm was encased in plaster. Maurice Edwards had extracted the bullet and worked hard at re-adjusting damaged bones and sinews and, upon his regaining consciousness, had proffered his prognosis; nothing he said had surprised the patient. Partial use of the arm would be regained but, unless Holbrook could suddenly become left-handed, his career as a lawman was over.

"Who?" he called.

"Supper," said Kate, opening the door.

"Confound it," he protested, as she toted a cloth-covered tray into his room. "I'm naked under these bedclothes — except for my right arm. Have you no delicacy, Mrs Preston?"

"That's how some folks would describe what I'm about to feed you," she said cheerfully, setting the tray on the bedside table. "Call me Kate. And now . . . "! She adjusted his pillows and helped him to a squatting position, "let's forget about what's under the bedclothes and get some nourishment into you."

"I'm not hungry," he grouched. "At least I wasn't until I caught the aroma of — what is that?"

"I call it Wolf Creek stew," she offered, perching on the edge of the bed. "The kids thrive on it. And you, Breck honey, could use some building up after all the blood you lost."

There followed some argument as to whether or not he could feed himself, but she had her way and, after his first few mouthfuls, he ceased to protest at her spoon-feeding him.

"That perfume . . . " he frowned when, a few moments later, she refilled the bowl.

"You mean me?" she asked. "I don't use perfume. All you're smelling is Kate Preston."

"And her great stew," he mumbled.

"Can I make a guess about that wound of yours? I haven't asked Doc Edwards. It's just a guess."

"All right — Kate. Make your guess."

"You won't be any use with a Colt from now on."

"Safe guess. I've already tendered my resignation to the mayor."

"You had to go to the mayor and . . . ?"

"That wasn't necessary." He downed another mouthful and confided with relish, "Cleave Archand looked in on me an hour ago. Accompanied by his so-proud wife, let me add, and the

263

Penns and the Meldrums. I've had quite a few other visitors, clients of the Reliance Bank, I presume. Duty visits, you know? The pariah is suddenly popular."

"Enough of your brooding," she chided. "We have to look to the future."

"We?" he frowned.

"Mister Meldrum would probably feel obliged to offer you a cashier's job," she opined.

"A sense of obligation," he nodded. "They're all feeling it now."

"But I can't imagine you'd want to go back to banking," she smiled, feeding him another spoonful. "Why not go further back, all the way back to ranching? You could do it, Breck. Wolf Creek needs a man's hand, and that goes double for Irma and Jarvis."

"Another proposal?" he challenged. "You certainly know how to take advantage of a bedridden prospect."

"Stop grouching," said Kate. "Give it some thought and, pretty soon, you'll

264

realize it's not such a wild idea. Very practical in fact. We'd get along, Breck. I've had five years to think only of my needs, but now . . . "

"But now?" he prodded.

"Believe it or not . . . " She flashed him another smile, "I find I'm suddenly concerned about *your* needs. And you know something? I think I'm enjoying it — fretting about somebody else. It must mean something, don't you think?"

"This," Holbrook fervently declared, "is a meal I'm not apt to forget."

On the law office porch, puffing on thinly-rolled cigarettes, the trouble-shooters traded hunches.

"I'd reckon a few more weeks," drawled Larry. "That's as long as we'll need to hang around Wolf Creek."

"There'll likely be a weddin'," Stretch said uneasily.

"Don't worry about it," soothed Larry. "I ain't forgettin' you always get choked up at weddin's."

"A weddin' is a nervous thing," muttered Stretch.

"We'll be gone from this territory before it happens," Larry promised.

"You think them Council Valley hombres gonna quit makin' trouble for the lady?" asked Stretch.

"That's what Aaron says," nodded Larry. "Seems Kipp and the Rockin' B boss did some hard talkin' to old McCord. My hunch is things'll be peaceable at the Preston spread from now on."

"Uh huh, well, this bullet-gash aches some, but my feet itch too," said Stretch. "So — soon as Doc says I can ride . . . ?"

"We'll ride," said Larry.

On their way out of Bridger County some weeks later, the on-the-loose Texans passed only one other traveler, an insurance salesman on his way to the county seat in response to an urgent summons from Emory Penn and Chester Meldrum.

CALABOOSE EXPRESS
WHISKEY GULCH
THE ALIBI TRAIL
SIX GUILTY MEN
FORT DILLON
IN PURSUIT OF QUINCEY BUDD
HAMMER'S HORDE
TWO GENTLEMEN FROM TEXAS
HARRIGAN'S STAR
TURN THE KEY ON EMERSON
ROUGH ROUTE TO RODD COUNTY
SEVEN KILLERS EAST
DAKOTA DEATH-TRAP
GOLD, GUNS AND THE GIRL
RUCKUS AT GILA WELLS
LEGEND OF COYOTE FORD
ONE HELL OF A SHOWDOWN
EMERSON'S HEX
SIX GUN WEDDING
THE GOLD MOVERS
WILD NIGHT IN WIDOW'S PEAK
THE TINHORN MURDER CASE
TERROR FOR SALE
HOSTAGE HUNTERS

TOP HAND
Wade Everett

The Broken T was big. But no ranch is big enough to let a man hide from himself.

GUN WOLVES OF LOBO BASIN
Lee Floren

The Feud was a blood debt. When Smoke Talbot found the outlaws who gunned down his folks he aimed to nail their hide to the barn door.

SHOTGUN SHARKEY
Marshall Grover

The westbound coach carrying the indomitable Larry and Stretch headed for a shooting showdown.

FIGHTING RAMROD
Charles N. Heckelmann

Most men would have cut their losses, but Frazer counted the bullets in his guns and said he'd soak the range in blood before he'd give up another inch of what was his.

LONE GUN
Eric Allen

Smoke Blackbird had been away too long. The Lequires had seized the Blackbird farm, forcing the Indians and settlers off, and no one seemed willing to fight! He had to fight alone.

THE THIRD RIDER
Barry Cord

Mel Rawlins wasn't going to let anything stand in his way. His father was murdered, his two brothers gone. Now Mel rode for vengeance.

ARIZONA DRIFTERS
W. C. Tuttle

When drifting Dutton and Lonnie Steelman decide to become partners they find that they have a common enemy in the formidable Thurston brothers.

TOMBSTONE
Matt Braun

Wells Fargo paid Luke Starbuck to outgun the silver-thieving stagecoach gang at Tombstone. Before long Luke can see the only thing bearing fruit in this eldorado will be the gallows tree.

HIGH BORDER RIDERS
Lee Floren

Buckshot McKee and Tortilla Joe cut the trail of a border tough who was running Mexican beef into Texas. They stopped the smuggler in his tracks.

BRETT RANDALL, GAMBLER
E. B. Mann

Larry Day had the choice of running away from the law or of assuming a dead man's place. No matter what he decided he was bound to end up dead.

THE GUNSHARP
William R. Cox

The Eggerleys weren't very smart. They trained their sights on Will Carney and Arizona's biggest blood bath began.

THE DEPUTY OF SAN RIANO
Lawrence A. Keating and
Al. P. Nelson

When a man fell dead from his horse, Ed Grant was spotted riding away from the scene. The deputy sheriff rode out after him and came up against everything from gunfire to dynamite.

FARGO: MASSACRE RIVER
John Benteen

The ambushers up ahead had now blocked the road. Fargo's convoy was a jumble, a perfect target for the insurgents' weapons!

SUNDANCE: DEATH IN THE LAVA
John Benteen

The Modoc's captured the wagon train and its cargo of gold. But now the halfbreed they called Sundance was going after it . . .

HARSH RECKONING
Phil Ketchum

Five years of keeping himself alive in a brutal prison had made Brand tough and careless about who he gunned down . . .

FARGO: PANAMA GOLD
John Benteen

With foreign money behind him, Buckner was going to destroy the Panama Canal before it could be completed. Fargo's job was to stop Buckner.

FARGO: THE SHARPSHOOTERS
John Benteen

The Canfield clan, thirty strong were raising hell in Texas. Fargo was tough enough to hold his own against the whole clan.

PISTOL LAW
Paul Evan Lehman

Lance Jones came back to Mustang for just one thing — revenge! Revenge on the people who had him thrown in jail.

HELL RIDERS
Steve Mensing

Wade Walker's kid brother, Duane, was locked up in the Silver City jail facing a rope at dawn. Wade was a ruthless outlaw, but he was smart, and he had vowed to have his brother out of jail before morning!

DESERT OF THE DAMNED
Nelson Nye

The law was after him for the murder of a marshal — a murder he didn't commit. Breen was after him for revenge — and Breen wouldn't stop at anything . . . blackmail, a frameup . . . or murder.

DAY OF THE COMANCHEROS
Steven C. Lawrence

Their very name struck terror into men's hearts — the Comancheros, a savage army of cutthroats who swept across Texas, leaving behind a bloodstained trail of robbery and murder.

SUNDANCE: SILENT ENEMY
John Benteen

A lone crazed Cheyenne was on a personal war path. They needed to pit one man against one crazed Indian. That man was Sundance.

LASSITER
Jack Slade

Lassiter wasn't the kind of man to listen to reason. Cross him once and he'll hold a grudge for years to come — if he let you live that long.

LAST STAGE TO GOMORRAH
Barry Cord

Jeff Carter, tough ex-riverboat gambler, now had himself a horse ranch that kept him free from gunfights and card games. Until Sturvesant of Wells Fargo showed up.

McALLISTER
ON THE
COMANCHE CROSSING
Matt Chisholm

The Comanche, McAllister owes them a life — and the trail is soaked with the blood of the men who had tried to outrun them before.

QUICK-TRIGGER COUNTRY
Clem Colt

Turkey Red hooked up with Curly Bill Graham's outlaw crew. But wholesale murder was out of Turk's line, so when range war flared he bucked the whole border gang alone . . .

CAMPAIGNING
Jim Miller

Ambushed on the Santa Fe trail, Sean Callahan is saved by two Indian strangers. But there'll be more lead and arrows flying before the band join Kit Carson against the Comanches.

GUNSLINGER'S RANGE
Jackson Cole

Three escaped convicts are out for revenge. They won't rest until they put a bullet through the head of the dirty snake who locked them behind bars.

RUSTLER'S TRAIL
Lee Floren

Jim Carlin knew he would have to stand up and fight because he had staked his claim right in the middle of Big Ike Outland's best grass.

THE TRUTH ABOUT SNAKE RIDGE
Marshall Grover

The troubleshooters came to San Cristobal to help the needy. For Larry and Stretch the turmoil began with a brawl and then an ambush.

WOLF DOG RANGE
Lee Floren

Will Ardery would stop at nothing, unless something stopped him first — like a bullet from Pete Manly's gun.

DEVIL'S DINERO
Marshall Grover

Plagued by remorse, a rich old reprobate hired the Texas Trouble-shooters to deliver a fortune in greenbacks to each of his victims.

GUNS OF FURY
Ernest Haycox

Dane Starr, alias Dan Smith, wanted to close the door on his past and hang up his guns, but people wouldn't let him.

DONOVAN
Elmer Kelton

Donovan was supposed to be dead. Uncle Joe Vickers had fired off both barrels of a shotgun into the vicious outlaw's face as he was escaping from jail. Now Uncle Joe had been shot — in just the same way.

CODE OF THE GUN
Gordon D. Shirreffs

MacLean came riding home, with saddle tramp written all over him, but sewn in his shirt-lining was an Arizona Ranger's star.

GAMBLER'S GUN LUCK
Brett Austen

Gamblers seldom live long. Parker was a hell of a gambler. It was his life — or his death . . .

ORPHAN'S PREFERRED
Jim Miller

Sean Callahan answers the call of the Pony Express and fights Indians and outlaws to get the mail through.

DAY OF THE BUZZARD
T. V. Olsen

All Val Penmark cared about was getting the men who killed his wife.

THE MANHUNTER
Gordon D. Shirreffs

Lee Kershaw knew that every Rurale in the territory was on the lookout for him. But the offer of $5,000 in gold to find five small pieces of leather was too good to turn down.

Doc Mike ——— e farmer stood there alone between Smith and Watson. There was this moment of stillness, and then the roar would start. And somebody would die . . .

HARTIGAN
Marshall Grover

Hartigan had come to Cornerstone to die. He chose the time and the place, and Main Street became a battlefield.

SUNDANCE: OVERKILL
John Benteen

When a wealthy banker's daughter was kidnapped by the Cheyenne, he offered Sundance $10,000 to rescue the girl.